The Spar Box

By Catherine Walker

To Jean,
Enjoy the read!
In Christ,
Catharine Kent Walker

1

Dedication

I thank God for my family and friends. I am grateful for their extensive knowledge and support. I also want to express a special thanks to my husband, for his assistance and encouragement.

Catherine Walker

thesparbox@gmail.com

Table of Contents

Prologue ~The Origins~

This book is dedicated to my ancestors who were involved in lead mining in Northern England. Around the turn of the century in 1800, they migrated to Southwest Virginia and continued mining there. One of the main settings for this story takes place in the Northern Pennine Mountains, in County Cumbria. Although this is a fictional story, I have tried to keep it as historically accurate as possible.

Long ago, volcanic eruptions and ever shifting glaciers created these mountains, leaving a distortion of cracks and faults in the underlying stone. As the heat and compression shifted, layers of slate were formed. Molten, igneous rock eventually formed huge masses of granite. Elements of limestone, shale, sandstone, and coal merged to form rich mineral deposits that included galena, the main source for lead, copper, zinc, barite, graphite, silver and gypsum. This array of land formations consisted of what the English call escarpments, fells, dales and moors, otherwise known as cliffs, hills, valleys and fields. The moors produced peat, covered with coarse grasses and moss; heather grew in abundance with purple, pink and white flowers accompanied by bilberry shrubs, gentian and primrose. Oak, birch, ash and hawthorn trees rose up on the land. There were plenty of animals, including red squirrels, grouse, pheasants, kestrel, raven, fox, badger, deer, cattle, sheep and horses.

The earliest record of lead mining was during the Roman rule of Northern England from 80 AD to the beginning of the 5th century. The Romans were known for lead mining and smelting. Lead was a byproduct of silver and gold ore refining. The Romans lined their aqueducts in lead. Cosmetics were lead-based. The cookware and wine vessels were made of lead. Lead was sweet tasting and enhanced the color and taste of wine. It was also used to sweeten foods. Lead poisoning was a disease of the rich in Roman times. Under the rule of Hadrian, the Roman legion built 73 miles of wall from east to west, much of it in the counties of Cumbria and Northumberland consisting of forts and mileposts built from the sandstones of the fells. Areas were mined close to the construction site of the forts as opposed to transporting iron from Spain or Greece.

Following the departure of the Romans and the advent of the Dark Ages, little is known about the mining history of the area until the Middle Ages. Evidence of mining has been documented by archeologists having found heaps of slag from iron smelting in the North Pennines. In the adjoining County of Durham, the earliest documentation of mining was evidenced in the 12th century when King Stephen granted mineral rights to his nephew Bishop Hugh Puiset in Weardale. Great sums of money were made leasing the mining rights by the Bishops of Durham. The church would take a royalty of 10% on the lead ore produced. In the 17th century, Sir William Blackett, acquired the lead mine leases and his family held the leases for the next two centuries until 1883 when the family (whose name had since changed to Beaumont) retired from the business due to increasing decline of profit. Not far down the road, one county over in Cumbria (known as Westmorland in the 1700s), in the 18th century, mineral rights were obtained by the Crown who had passed them down to the Royal Hospital for Seaman at Greenwich. There was another major lead mining Company, The London Lead Company, formed by Quakers in 1692 and they leased from the Greenwich Hospital and managed mines in the Northern Pennines. There were many small lead mines that were mined privately prior to the formation of the lead companies. The Lewis' were one such family.

The beginnings of the Lewis family are found in the church registry of the Long Marton Parish of St. Margaret and St. James. The earliest reference to the existence of this Roman Catholic Church was the 13th century. The initial burial registries were from the late 16th century. Families from Long Marton, Knock and Brampton attended this church. Residents of Long Marton were involved in lead and silver mining in the 12th century as evidenced by accounts at the Royal Mint for making coinage in the nearby town of Carlisle and most worked at the Dufton Fell Mine. Dufton Fell is one of the tallest points in the Northern Pennines at 2,779 feet After the church of St. Cuthbert was established in nearby Dufton (part of the same benefice as Long Marton) many families moved there for proximity. This church's namesake, St. Cuthbert is said to have brought Christianity to the area in the 7th century.

Chapter 1~ The Blairs 2012~

I don't give a rip about family heritage, but to my mother, digging up the dead is her life. I thought to myself as I was driving home from Emory University   for summer break. My parents have invited me to accompany them to Virginia to visit my brother, Austin. He manages a riding academy and is active in the Tennessee Walking Horse show circuit. At age 25, Austin remains a bachelor and lives in the Venable family home place (my mother's side) was plantation before the Civil War. While cleaning out the attic one day, he found a several old journals in a box, written by our great, great, great -grandmother, Hannah Lewis Venable. Knowing Mom loved discovering more about our genealogy, he invited my parents up for a visit for a few weeks. I suppose there is some merit in knowing your ancestors, but why waste my time on just my family's history. Being an art history major, I prefer history through the detailed creation of artists. Their lives are far more fascinating to study than the boring endeavors of our families. But, I am in need of some rest and relaxation before beginning my sophomore year, so I decided to tag along.

It seemed my family was born to have some unique Southern heritage. I couldn't help but wonder what secrets were in those memoirs. I was so engulfed in my thoughts that my cell phone rang several times before I came back to reality to answer it. "Talk to me," I insisted.

"Aspen?" "I wish you wouldn't answer the phone that way!"

"Hi, Mom," I responded.

"How soon will you get to town?" she queried.

"I just turned off on the Gainesville exit," I answered.

"That's great. I'll have dinner ready by the time you get here", she said.

"I hope we're having barbeque".

"Dad is putting the chicken on the grill now. See you in a bit. Love ya."

"Love ya, bye".

A few minutes later, I pulled into the driveway to the house where I had lived since I was born, 20 years ago. The large, red, brick, split-level style home welcomed me with a surge of warm memories as I gathered my overnight bag. Climbing up the steps to the front porch, I remembered the times we had rocked ourselves to sleep on warm, summer evenings, sipping iced tea. Opening the front door, I stepped inside. Walking through the living room, I reminisced about the last time I was here during the holidays. We always had a live Christmas tree placed in front of the large, picture window that faces the street. I loved the fragrance of the evergreen and the aroma of baking cookies. I couldn't avoid my image in the large, gold leaf mirror hanging over the couch that welcomed all visitors, reflecting their mood as they passed through the room. My shoulder-length, brown hair was windblown from driving with my windows down. If the mirror could talk, she would thank me for greeting her without streaks of blue, red, or other colors of hair. I had matured since my punk and gothic years in high school.

"Mom, Dad, "I'm here, and I'm starved!" I yelled.

Mom came out of the kitchen. She never seemed to change. People often mistook us sisters. Even though Mom was almost 50, she kept her figure trim. We hugged and she welcomed me home, "Aspen, good to see you; go put your things in your room and wash up. Dinner is ready".

My childhood room looks exactly the same as I left it a year ago. Even though I had only been away from home a year, I feel much older. Peering through the open window, I saw Dad taking the chicken off the grill. I could smell the wonderful aroma of barbeque sauce that permeated the air. Dad wore shorts and a polo shirt covered by a full-length, white apron that said 'Kiss the Cook' in black letters on the bib. His short, black hair was starting to gray around the temples. He wore black-rimmed glasses; I always thought this made him look very distinguished, even in casual clothes. Dad was several years older than Mom, but also looked good for his age. I knocked on the window, waved and said hello. He responded with a big smile, waving the spatula at me.

While I was unpacking my bag, I thought about how my parents met. Mom went on vacation to Myrtle Beach with her cousins. They met my future Dad, Cecil, in the motel lobby while waiting to check in. He struck up a conversation with them and discovered they needed a fourth person for bridge. Mom and Dad hit it off and after several years of long distance romance, they were married.

On their first anniversary, they planned a snow skiing trip to Aspen, Colorado. They flew to Denver and rented a car, deciding to take a scenic route. They arrived in the little town of Austin. They were snowed in because of a record snowfall and never made it to Aspen. Nine months later, my brother was born and my Mom named him after that little town. Five years later, they decided to go to Aspen again for their anniversary. This time they made it there and nine months later, I was born. There must be something about those towns that begin with 'A" in Colorado. Mom broke my reverie, and called out from downstairs, "Dinner is ready Aspen". I ambled down the stairs.

As I entered the dining room, Dad met me at the door and gave me a big hug and said "It is so good to see you!" Mom was already seated and he motioned me to sit down. As customary, we held hands and Dad returned thanks to the Lord.

13

"I'm glad you are taking the summer off, Dad," I exclaimed. Dad was a retired Professor of Theology and taught some classes at the local community college. Mom had worked as a court reporter while Dad finished his Master's Degree. She was able to quit working after Dad started his teaching career.

"Yes, since I won't be teaching any courses, we can stay in Virginia for the whole summer!" he replied.

Mom added, "We are all packed and ready to leave in the morning. I can't wait to see the journals that Austin found."

It took about seven hours to make the trip to Max Meadows, Virginia. We departed right after a quick breakfast of coffee and blueberry muffins. We took I-85 and traveled through South and North Carolina to Charlotte and got onto I-77 to Virginia. We took the exit for the Historic Shot Tower, crossing New River. Dad honked his horn as he turned into the driveway of the old Venable Home. Austin was in the back yard, mowing the grass. He resembled Indiana Jones, wearing khaki pants and button up shirt and even that classic hat. Stopping the mower, he came over to greet us. "Hi Mom and Dad, hey Lil Sis " as he waved to us, "Let's get your things out of the car and we'll sit in the sun room and I'll get you some sweet tea." Mom jumped out of the car and gave him a big hug. She hadn't seen him in several years.

That sounded great to me. We unloaded the car moved our luggage into the guest bedrooms, and settled in the huge sun room on the back side of the house facing the mountains. I plopped into one of the two matching white wicker chairs. Mom and Dad snuggled into the matching a couch. Austin delivered a cool pitcher of ice tea on the wrought iron and glass coffee table in front of the furniture, facing the mountains. An array of indoor plants lined the large paned windows.

"Let's see that box!" said Mom, wasting no time to view its contents.

Austin walked over to a table near the couch, picked up the wooden container and handed it to Mom, "I knew you wouldn't want to wait to see this. Dad, will you come into the kitchen with me to help start dinner while the girls look at the journals?" Dad, believing he was a master chef, was always willing to help out. So he jumped at the chance to help prepare a meal.

Mom held the box in her lap and said, "Aah, this looks like the "Hannah Box" my mother spoke of when I was younger. It is handmade from walnut." The delicately hinged top was covered with a piece of tattered needlepoint; we examined the blue and white striped material underneath the handiwork which served as a large pin cushion. Each side of the lid rendered these inscriptions: On the front edge- Made for Hannah Lewis Venable, on the right side – By Senah Newell Venable in her

15

fifty-ninth year, and on the left side – Finished August 12, 1848. I asked, "Who was Senah Newell Venable?"

Mom replied, "Hannah's husband, John, was Senah's great-nephew. She and Senah were very close".

"How in the world to you keep up with these names?"

"Your grandmother and her sisters kept handwritten family lists and I transcribed them into a family tree with a computer program." Mom opened the box and said, "Look Aspen, it is full of old booklets!" Each diary consisted of pages of lined paper, browned with age, and folded in the middle, with string threaded in the crease.

Austin popped his head into the room, "I haven't read through the journals, but you may want to sort them out, Mom. It looks as if Hannah dated each front page by year. I figured you'd want to read them in chronological order."

"Yes, Austin thanks. Aspen, let's sort this literature into some piles."

"Sounds good Mom", so we sorted them by year. The earlier journals were a compilation of stories that Hannah's mom, Anne, had told her about their family history in England. The later journals included daily entries; each one spanning over six months.

"Aspen, why don't you take this one to read?" suggested Mom showing me the oldest booklet dated back to 1826.

"Okay, I'll start on it tonight before I go to bed". The old, worn pages and aged narratives of these journals ignited a spark of interest in our family history.

"Time to eat!" Dad yelled from the kitchen. We went into the kitchen which Austin remodeled recently, and we enjoyed steaks, baked potatoes, along with Greek salad, rolls and coconut cake. Mom, Dad and Austin retired to the den after dinner with coffee and started catching up on events of Austin's life.

I actually couldn't wait to begin reading the journal and excused myself for the evening. Even though it was June, a cool breeze filled the air that evening; so I opened the window and listened to the cicadas (what I called kaydidids as a child). Then, I nestled into the antique Lincoln bed with a sea of goose-down pillows surrounding me. After reading my devotion, I picked up the delicate journal. The pages were stiff. Hannah wrote with pencil in script and the words had faded with age. The first page notated the year, 1826 in large letters, and underneath it said, written by Hannah Lewis Venable, and underneath that, was written, age 20. I turned the page and began reading.

Chapter 2 ~Excerpts from Hannah Lewis' Journal~

January 1, 1826 One year ago today, my husband and I were married. John and I just could not wait any longer. On New Year's Eve, I traveled to see my cousins, Sarah and Deborah, who live across the river. Aware of my intentions to elope, they let me hide in their room all day. They slipped portions of their dinner to me after supper. We all went to bed and just before the sunrise. John threw a rock at my window. I climbed out the window and by the time we got to the hack, I realized I had left my gloves. They were very dear to me because it was a gift from Mama. I had to go get them and at the risk of waking up my cousin's family; I climbed back through the window, got my gloves, and slipped back out the window, running back to the hack. We traveled about 40 miles to Mount Airy, North Carolina, just over the Virginia state line. John had a friend whose father was a Justice of the Peace, and we arrived at his house about 1:00 PM and exchanged our wedding vows. We got back in the hack, and rode back to Max Meadows about 10:00 PM. Thank goodness the weather was mild for January, or I would have frozen. John brought me back to the Newby's house. I stole into the house again through my cousin's window. I had to tell Sarah and Deborah all about our trip, but we had to be quiet, so as not to wake their folks. The next morning, out I went through that window and met John at the Shot Tower. We bravely drove the hack back to my house and broke the news to Mama and Papa. I thought they would be mad, they loved John and, though they were taken by surprise, they wished us well. Since several of John's brothers had moved to Missouri, John had a room to himself and his parents let us move in with them.

February 5, 1826 I am 20 years-old today. Mama and Papa invited John and me over for lunch. She cooked salt-cured ham, mashed potatoes and gravy, peas and carrots, salt-rising bread and a chocolate birthday cake. My younger brother, George, and my older stepbrother, Robert, were there. Mama gave me with a beautiful blue and green blanket that she had woven. Papa and my brothers presented me with a cedar chest; they built it together! John surprised me and gave me a necklace with a small diamond pendant. He said he had been saving up his money and bought it on a trip to Richmond.

*May 9, 1826*I hadn't been feeling well lately. I thought I might have a sick stomach. I had been throwing up a lot. John had gone to Richmond again with my Uncle Thomas, so Mama took me to the doctor in Wytheville. He asked me some questions, and then he told me that he thought that I would be having a baby in about six months. I cannot wait to tell John when he gets home. Mama was full of excitement. She said that she would have to help me make some bigger dresses to make room for a growing baby. I am so thankful Mama lives nearby.

Chapter 3 ~The Shot Tower~

I awoke around 9 AM, stretched out my arms, and rubbed the sleep from my eyes. The aroma of the coffee and bacon wafted upstairs to my room, beckoning me to get to breakfast. I ran my fingers through my askew hair, got out of bed, and padded down the stairs, still in my PJs. Mom always woke up earlier than the rest of the house, and prepared breakfast. She was sitting at the bar in the kitchen, sipping coffee, and reading the newspaper.

"Morning Glory", Mom said.

"Morning," I responded, still groggy as I grabbed a mug and poured some coffee.

"Did you happen to read the journal? Mom queried.

"Yes. I enjoyed reading about Hannah. She was about my age, you know."

"Last night, I read the letter that Hannah's mother, Anne, wrote in 1825, depicting her journey to America. Would you like to swap journals?" Mom asked.

I considered this briefly. "Okay, I'll trade with you after breakfast".

We chatted more about the journals as we finished our breakfast of bacon and English Muffins slathered with butter and grape jelly. Afterwards, I went back upstairs to shower and wash my hair. I recently restyled my hair with bangs for the first time since second grade. My natural, dark brown hair featured the last of my blonde streaks feathering at the tips of my bangs. My hair continually endures all sorts of styles and colors. I'll probably add a blue streak before long, not to be mundane. I slipped on a pair of jeans and a T-shirt and started down the stairs. About halfway down, I remembered the journal. I knew Mom would already have her journal in hand for the trade, so I ran back to the room and retrieved Hannah's narrative.

By this time, Austin was downstairs finishing his breakfast. "Hi sis, want to do some horseback riding today?"

"Of course!" I loved to ride and only had the opportunity when I visited Austin.

"Alrighty then, I'll meet you at the barn after I eat and get changed." Austin replied as he yawned and scratched his head.

Mom must have gone back to the bedroom, so I left the booklet on the kitchen counter and ventured outside. The air was still crisp with the dew just drying on the grass. Austin's two black Labrador retrievers, Bandit and Smokey, met me at the porch, both tails wagging uncontrollably. After giving both dogs ample attention, I walked to the barn, and the dogs followed along.

Austin had four Tennessee Walking Horses which he rotated riding in horse shows. He had a room full of trophies and ribbons. He also owned two horses for trail riding. He purchased Apache, an Appaloosa and Quarter Horse mix, because he was gentle, and willingly entered a horse trailer without complications. Austin's show horses balked at riding in the trailer. However, when he led Apache in the trailer first, then the other horses would calmly enter in. Of all my brother's horses, Gypsy, a Morgan Horse, will always be my favorite. She had five gaits; one was racking, like his show horses. Gypsy was an excellent trail horse, as long as she was the leader.

Entering into the barn with the two dogs, the appealing smell of the hay instantly hit my nostrils. The bales stacked up almost to the rafters across from the stalls. Naturally, there were other odors that were not as likable in the stalls! Several of the horses whinnied to welcome me. They also knew it was breakfast time. I scooped some grain from the barrel just inside the barn door and poured a small portion into the troughs in each stall.

About that time, the dogs started barking because they saw Austin walking to the barn. He whistled to them and they ran toward him because they knew there were doggie cookies in

Austin's pocket. Smokey and Bandit immediately sat at his feet, waiting for their treat. "It's about time you got here. I've already fed the horses", I remarked.

"That's great!" he said as he crossed over to the tack room. "Pick out your gear for the day, and I'll see if Gypsy is finished eating her grain. Austin kept English and Western tack since he had friends who liked to ride Western, especially on overnight trail rides. I could ride either way, but I preferred English; I felt more in tune with my horse. The sheer bulk of Western gear makes the riding experience more difficult for me. I made my selection and removed the saddle and bridle from their racks. Austin had already secured Gypsy's halter to the ropes, placing her in the center of the barn walkway. As he finished brushing her coat, he helped me place the saddle on her back. After cinching the girth strap, I replaced her halter with a bridle. I led her out of the barn and tied the reins to the fence adjacent to the barn. I had retrieved some sugar cubes from the kitchen, placed them in my palm and offered them to Gypsy. She gently ate them. I ambled back to the barn and helped Austin gear up Apache.

As we were saddling up, I asked, "Where are we going today?"

"We are going to visit the old Shot Tower, and a relative whom you have never met."

I replied, "Sounds interesting, I'm ready to go!"

We took a leisurely ride, crossing the footbridge over the New River. We trotted down a path, parallel to the old railroad track along the river's edge. The temperature was cool in the shade of the old oak trees that draped our trail like a canopy. At one point, we rode by what looked like an earthen cave dug out of the hillside. Obscured by undergrowth and muscadine grapevines that dangled from the huge oak trees, the cave seemed welcoming in a mysterious sort of way. The vines were so thick that you could swing on them   "Do you know anything about this cave?" I asked my brother.

"As a matter of fact, I do", Austin explained; then, he cocked his head smirking at me saying, "But seeing how you find family history so dull, I wouldn't want to bore you with the details."

I pondered his comment for a moment and replied, "Reading the journal last night sparked an interest in my family history. Please tell me about the cave, if it involves our family."

"Why don't we stop here and give the horses a rest, and I'll give you a little history lesson", Austin said. We dismounted and he grabbed two bottles of water from his knapsack. He found an old log and as we plopped down on it, Austin began his narration.

"As you know, the house where I live used to belong to our great- grandparents. The original home place was across the road on the New River bottom land and it was washed away in a flood in 1878. Across the river, was the Newell land that had been in the family since Thomas Newell came over from England around 1795. He built the house that is currently standing, along with several thousand acres. Thomas was the uncle of Hannah, author of the journal.

Thomas was a very prosperous businessman and managed the lead mines in the area." Austin took a long sip of water and continued, "At the crest of the hill above us is an old historical monument called the "Shot Tower". Thomas died while the shot tower was being built in 1824. Robert Graham, his nephew by his sister's first marriage, completed the project. Most shot towers were made of brick, but this one is made of limestone. The walls are about two feet thick. The building is about 125 feet tall, and, at that time, included a 50 foot shaft that descended to the river. The tower has a wooden stairway that winds around the inside walls to a room at the top which is about four feet square."

"Wow, that sounds neat, a winding staircase, can we go up in the tower?" I interrupted.

"Yes, it has been renovated, so it is not original anymore; the steps are metal now with handrails for safety. After the Newell's donated that portion of land where the Shot Tower stands to the State of Virginia, the interior was renovated for safety." Austin continued his story, "Anyway, there was a furnace in the corner where the lead was melted and the molten lead was placed in a colander that was in the center of the room. The lead dropped through the colander the distance of the 50 foot shaft into a tub of water where it cooled into balls of shot or bullets that were used for firearms. That cave over there is actually the opening to the tunnel that goes about 100 feet to the base of the shaft where the tubs of water that cooled the shot. The shot was retrieved from the tubs and taken out though the tunnel. At that point, the shot was bundled up and ready for sale."

I had another question, "Can we go into the tunnel?"

"I'm afraid not, it has been blocked off with a metal gate, again for safety's sake," Austin replied. "Years ago, when the shot tower was in operation, one of the workers was hauling out a batch of the cooled shot out of the tunnel, a pile of rocks came lose from the shaft and fell on the worker's head, killing him. The Newell family arranged for his burial and bought a farm for his wife and family."

I said, "Well, that was awfully nice of the Newells."

"Yes, they were very benevolent folks and took care of their employees. Do you see that road over there?" Austin asked as he pointed across the river. "It used to be the main road from North Carolina. Men would come here, cross the river using the ferry, then buy the shot right near the ferry at a "Shot Shop". The shot was also distributed up north by the train that stopped in Wytheville.

Austin added, "A little known fact is that during the War Between the States or, as descendants of the Confederacy call it, the War of Northern Aggression, ammunition for the Confederate Army mostly came from here. In fact, three battles were fought in this area; the Union army tried to either destroy or gain control of the mines.

"Wow, now that was an interesting story! It tempts me to read more of the journals!" I exclaimed.

As we continued our ride, Austin said, "The Old Newell home place is just across the pasture. That is our next stop."

Chapter 4 ~Rose Graham Evans~

We cantered across the pasture, bringing the horses to a halt, then carefully crossed the highway and turned into the driveway. The white, two-story, antebellum home was tucked beneath massive pecan trees. We dismounted and tied the reins to the picket fence next to the garage. A spacious porch wrapped around the front of the home. I admired the row of high back rocking chairs with wicker seats.

As we climbed the steps to the porch, an elderly woman opened the front door. She was short in stature with a head of silver hair. Her eyes were bright blue. She wore denim jeans and a red T-shirt. "Hello Rose, "said Austin.

"How are you, Austin?" replied Rose. "What brings you here on another beautiful day that the Lord made?"

"My sister and I were just out riding and I thought you two would like to meet. Rose, this is Aspen. Aspen, this is Rose."

I reached out for a handshake; Rose approached with arms opened wide, and gave me a big embrace. "Hello Aspen. My, my, aren't you lovely!" She eyed me then Austin. "I can certainly tell that you two are related. You all are definitely two peas from the same pod."

I smiled and said, "Yes, that's what people tell us. It is so nice to meet you."

Rose asked, "Do you all have time to come in for some iced tea and homemade cookies?"

Before I had a chance to speak, Austin replied, "We sure do."

"Well, come on inside," replied Rose. We entered the foyer. The house was just as pretty on the inside as it was on the outside. To the right of the foyer was a living room. I quickly peeked in. A fireplace was on one side of the room and a baby grand piano was on the opposite side. In the center of the room were two overstuffed sofas facing one another. Between them was a coffee table with a vase of fresh-cut red tiger lilies. Over the fireplace was an ornately-framed painting. I left Austin and Rose, venturing over to view the painting up close which was an original watercolor. It was a landscape of an island, my guess, in the Caribbean. I completed a course in American artists which included Winslow Homer. He was famous for his landscapes, seascapes and animal watercolors. I remember reading that he took his paper, brushes and colors with him when he traveled. He did some landscape paintings while in Florida and the Caribbean. "Rose," I called out, "Do you know anything about this painting?"

Rose and Austin walked into the room, "Well, dear," Rose said as she examined the painting, putting her forefinger to her temple," I don't know much about this painting except that it belonged to my great-great grandfather, Robert Graham." She sat down on the sofa. "I have a drawer upstairs that contains some old family letters that have been passed down over the years. Maybe they can be of help." She arose from the couch, "Let me serve you the cookies first."

We crossed over into the hallway and entered the dining room. In the center of the room was a mahogany Victorian table and eight chairs.   In the corner was a beautiful sideboard and matching china cabinet, full of ornate, china, crystal and various knickknacks.

We entered the kitchen. It had obviously been remodeled as it contained modern stainless, steel appliances. In the breakfast nook was an oblong, maple table with padded chairs with a large bay window that overlooked Rose's flower garden. One would think that Rose's flower garden was full of roses, but no, her garden was a multitude of lilies. "Your lilies are beautiful!" I exclaimed as I looked out the window at the array of colors and varieties. "Lilies are my favorite flower". Rose walked to the table with a plate full of cookies, still warm from the oven and set them on the table. Austin dug in with both hands, eating the cookies.

"Why thank you, Aspen," Rose replied, "As you can see, they are my favorite flower, as well. You see, my mother named me Rose, because that was her favorite blossom, especially pink blossoms. My room was painted pink, and she dressed me in pink while I was young. I don't particularly care for roses, and

31

I don't like the color pink; but my mother did teach me how to raise plants and cultivate hybrids. That I did grow to love, no pun intended. When I was younger, I looked forward to June when the orange day lilies bloomed and grew along the roadside. Mom and I attended a garden show one time, and there were a variety of lilies on display. I knew then and there when I grew up that I would have a garden of these unique flowers."

Rose went back into the kitchen and returned with ice tea served with a sprig of mint. "If you have time after our snack, I'll show you around the garden," Rose offered.

"Oh, yes, I'd love to," I replied, as I sipped the iced tea. After Rose was assured that we were satisfied, she stated, "Ya'll enjoy yourselves and I'll go fetch that box."

It didn't take long for Rose to return with a small drawer and set it down on the table. "I remember reading something about that painting." She sifted through the old documents until she found the one she wanted. My great-great grandfather wrote letters to his wife whenever he traveled." She opened the letter and began perusing it. "This letter is dated the 24 August 1885." She skimmed down the paper, "Ah, here we go.... Today, I visited our good friend, Trip Kincannon, in Miami. In his company was a Mr. Winslow Homer, an artist from New York, who had just returned from a trip to several islands off the coast of Florida in the Caribbean Sea. Mr. Homer had with him some watercolor paintings of the islands. I was quite taken with his work. I asked him if I could purchase a piece of his artwork. He was quite happy to let me select my favorite painting. I hope you can find a nice place to hang it in our house." Rose read down through the letter. "That's all there is about the painting".

"That's freaking' awesome!" I exclaimed

"Is he famous?" Austin added.

"Are you kidding? He is one of the great American artists. I wish I owned a Winslow Homer. His art hangs in places like The National Gallery of Art in Washington, D.C., The Metropolitan Museum of Art in New York, and even in Paris."

Rose said to me, "Where did you hear about Winslow Homer?"

"I am pursuing a degree in art history."

Then Rose added, "I think I have something else you may be interested in." She left the kitchen again and shortly returned, holding a sculpture made of metal and wire and handed it to me. It was an image of a person of some sort. "Did you make this?"

Rose sat down at the table. "No, I didn't," she replied. "When I was in college in New York, I roomed with a girl named Mary Calder."

"Calder, that name sounds familiar."

"We were close friends and I would frequently go home with her on the weekends; her parents lived in New York. Mary's father was an artist.

"You don't mean her father was the artist, Alexander Calder?" I asked excitedly.

Rose replied, "Yes, his name was Alexander, though his friends and family called him Sandy." She continued her story, "One evening, her father was performing his Cirque Calder for a benefit dinner and he invited Mary and me to attend. He acted out a circus show with animals and characters made of wood and wire. It was most fascinating.

Austin had a perplexed look on his face and asked, "What is a Cirque Calder?"

Rose explained, "Mr. Calder sculpted circus animals and people out of wire. They were fully functional to do small tricks. For instance, the clowns had hooks in their hands and they rolled down a wire and could land on a horse. The animals had moveable parts. He was situated in the middle of the circus and performed the acts with his interactive sculptures. They were more like toys than a work of art. Later that year at Christmas, Mr. Calder gave me this sculpture of an acrobat."

"Wow, that figure must be worth a fortune!" I exclaimed, and gently placed the figure on the table.

"Maybe," Rose answered, "but I would never sell it." Then Rose changed the subject. "So what brings you to visit God's country?"

"Austin invited us up because he found a box full of diaries and journals written by our grandmother's grandmother, or something like that. He wanted our mother to have a look at them since she is really into family history. Mom saw it as a chance for the family to get together; we hadn't seen Austin in a while, so she asked me to come, too."

Rose inquired, "Have you read any of them?"

"I have read one, written by Hannah somebody."

Austin cut in between mouthfuls of cookies, "Hannah Lewis Venable," and continued eating.

"Yes," I agreed, "and Mother read one last night written by Anne Lewis, Hannah's mother."

"Interesting," Rose replied, "Anne Lewis was my fourth great-grandmother.

"Really? Then doesn't that make us related?" I questioned Rose.

"Well, sort of," Rose explained," Anne's brother was Thomas Newell, who built this house. Anne's first husband was William Graham, and I descend from them. After William died, she married Richard Lewis. You and Austin descend from her second marriage."

I nodded in agreement.

By this time, Austin had finished his snack and said, "That's too complicated for me." He turned to me and said, "Most of the folks who live in this county are cousins. Rose, thanks for the cookies and tea. I'm going to go check on the horses." He rose from the table, dabbed his mouth with the linen napkin Rose had provided, bent over to give Rose a kiss on the cheek, and left the room.

"Would you like to take a stroll out to the backyard? Rose asked.

"I've been waiting for you to ask. Let's go!" I said as I gathered the dishes from the table and carried them to the kitchen counter. Rose directed me to the kitchen door that opened to a beautiful deck. There were a set of stairs that led down to the back yard. We entered the flower garden through a trellis. The garden was enclosed by a chain link fence; I imagined this was to keep animals out of her plants. "It's taken me years to get this garden just the way I want it," Rose explained.

The garden had a pebbled path that meandered throughout the lilies. In the center of the garden was an enclosed gazebo that served as a hub for the various trails. As we walked through the flowers, I could identify my favorites. There were oriental lilies with petals of dark pink with white outlines, white trumpet lilies, and my favorites, tiger lilies of various colors including yellow and fuchsia. There was a patch of smaller crinum lilies of purple, pink and white. There was also a section of snow white, lily of the valley variety. Bordering the garden were dark and light orange day lilies. Since it was June, many of the lilies were in bloom. Pointing to a cluster of plants, I asked Rose, "There are several here I can't identify."

Rose described, "In this patch are ginger lilies. They bloom in late summer and early fall. They are white and smell like honeysuckle." We kept walking, "Over here", Rose directed me to a beautiful yellow variety. "These are glacier lilies. My favorite lily is the stargazer lily," she said, as we approached another section of flowers. The blooms were purple with black dots in the petals, with thin white edges.

"How many varieties of lilies to you have?" I queried.

"Let me think," Rose pondered, "Last count, including hybrids... I have twenty-five species now. I get to enjoy bouquets of lilies from early June until late in September. These flowers are from God's palate. He is the Master Painter. I just don't understand how people can say there is no God, when all you have to do is look at nature to see His handiwork."

I had to agree with Rose. We finished walking around the garden as Austin walked up to the back gate of the garden, "Hey, Sis, it's getting late, we need to saddle up!"

I turned to Rose, "Thank you so much for such a wonderful afternoon. It was so nice to meet you. I hope we meet again before I leave".

"The pleasure was all mine," returned Rose, "it's not every day that I meet a new relative! Enjoy the rest of your ride. Bye now, Austin."

"Bye Rose, and thanks again for the refreshments," said Austin.

We mounted up and ambled down the driveway and crossed the road to the pasture. "Rose sure is a nice lady," I said," Do you see her often?"

"Yes, I check in on her several times a week. She knows to call me if she needs anything fixed around the house. I even do her yard work for her."

"So, what is her story?" I asked.

"Mom knows a lot more about her than I do," he replied.

Austin didn't offer anymore information about Rose. I decided I'd talk to Mom later on this evening. We rode back to the barn. As I dismounted, I realized the muscles in my legs were aching. It had been a long time since I had ridden. I was ready for a long, hot shower.

After dinner, Mom was relaxing, sitting on the back porch. We discussed the events of the day, "So tell me about Rose, Mom."

Mom reminisced, "When I was born, Rose was in college in New York. I think she went to Columbia University. She got her degree in botany. She met and married Adam Evans shortly after she graduated. She was a teacher in a private school and he was a lawyer. They would come down here to visit her family every Christmas and we were always invited for Christmas dinner." Mom stopped and smiled, "Rose always brought me the best gifts!" She continued, "Rose and Adam had a home in the country with a large pond. They loved to go ice skating. When I was about ten, Adam died in a freak accident."

"What happened?"

"Adam and Rose had left the house to go skating on their pond. Rose heard the phone ring and returned to answer it. Adam proceeded to the pond. When Rose got back to the pond, Adam had fallen through a thin spot in the ice. He was

39

struggling desperately to climb out, but each time he pulled himself out, another piece of ice would break. Rose tried to get him out, but he feared that she would fall in, too. She found a length of rope and tied it to a nearby tree and threw it out to Adam to grab onto, hoping that he could pull himself closer to shore and get out of the cold water. She ran back to the house and called for help. The rescue workers arrived and were able to pull Adam out of the pond. Unfortunately, he suffered hypothermia and died shortly thereafter.

"How sad," I broke in, "Did they have any children?"

"No. Rose regarded her students as her children," Mom answered." It turned out that Adam was quite wealthy. He had invested in stocks and of course, Rose was the beneficiary. Rose finished out the school year and decided to move back to Virginia, living with her parents and taking care of them until they died. She inherited the place where she now lives. Rose is very benevolent. She continues to donate to college scholarship funds to the local high schools."

I gave Mom a hug and said, "Well, that's about it for me today, I'm pretty beat from all the stuff we did this afternoon. I think I'll turn in and read that letter that Anne wrote her daughter. Good night."

"I think I'll sit out here for a while longer," replied Mom, "good night."

Chapter 5~ Anne's Newell Lewis's Letter

April 10, 1825

My Dearest Hannah,

When you told me that you were expecting, I decided to pen a letter to you. You may not take an interest in this now, but I want you have knowledge about our family history.

I was raised in Dufton, England, with two brothers and two sisters, I was in the middle. My father was a lead miner and a farmer. We went to church every Sunday at Long Marton Parish. My brother, John, followed in my father's footsteps and my older brother, Thomas, learned the blacksmith and tool maker trade from his uncle. Thomas's intelligence aided him in advancing to a lead mining manager. He worked diligently and journeyed around Northern England to various mines, supplying them with tools and instructing the workers on more efficient ways to mine.

Thomas met Moses and Stephen Austin, brothers from Virginia who were seeking to gain knowledge about the English mining and smelting methods. They were so impressed with him, they suggested that he travel to America and supervise their mining endeavors in Virginia. Moses Austin and his family later moved to Missouri to pursue mining. Moses received a grant of land in Texas and shortly afterward, died, leaving the grant to his son, Stephen, who went on to help in the colonization of that land.

Papa had an uncle who was quite wealthy from his shipping business. My father was his favorite nephew. He never married. When he died, Papa was the sole heir in his will and he inherited a great deal of money. Papa split the money with all of his children. My portion was used to get an education and I became a school teacher. Thomas was going to use his measure to pay for his passage to America, purchase a tract of land and construct a home. He left England in 1793 when he was 31, due to some rather unfortunate circumstances. He settled here in Wythe County, working for the Austins for several years and then he decided to lease the mines after the Austins moved away.

I met William Graham, a tradesman from Liverpool. My brother bought goods from William, and they became friends. William travelled to the villages of Dufton and Knock selling raw materials to the local smithies. We were married one year later in Long Marton Parish in 1789.

After our first child, Robert, was born, William decided to return to Liverpool. I was tired of the countryside and wanted to see the big city, so I agreed to move with him. We lived in a pleasant home in the city. We moved several times as William's business grew and our family grew as well. By the time your *sister, Mary, was born in 1796, we were living in a fine house on McGuire Street.*

In 1801, we received a letter from Thomas about the prosperity of the lead mining industry in Virginia. His description of the land seemed so inviting that William decided to sell all we had and move to Virginia. Thomas wrote to his brother, John and invited him to come with us. John and William then persuaded other miners, smelters and tradesmen to move to Virginia to work in the lucrative lead mines.

William had a friend who owned the ship, Phoenix, berthed in Liverpool. He conversed with the Captain regarding booking passage. His negotiations were successful and our family and several others from Dufton, obtained tickets.

William visited the docks and inspected the Phoenix as the crew was stocking her to go to America. The quays were full of people who lived in various regions of England, looking for passage to various ports across the Atlantic. We were busy gathering provisions for the voyage expecting to take at least twelve weeks. We stocked jugs of water, containers of coffee, sugar, ham, potatoes, eggs and flour. The ship had to provide a means to cook our food.

The day came when we boarded the ship. The Phoenix was a brig that had three masts with square sails. Many of the men and boys were helping the crew with the rigging. Of course, our boys wanted to go help, but I was fearful they would get hurt. The Phoenix was a cargo ship and was altered to carry passengers. Temporary floors had been added below the main deck and upper and lower berths were built in the cargo area.

As we left the port, people from shore waved and cheered well-wishes. We stood on the deck, returning the gesture, as the wind filled the sails. I had never been on a ship before and it was exciting. The weather was beautiful. Once the sails were set and decks were cleared, the Captain ordered all of the passengers to stand on the deck for a muster. We had already stored our baggage in our assigned berth below. The captain checked the passengers off; making sure everyone had already paid for their passage. Once accounted for, the person or groups of people were sent back below. When the muster was completed, everyone was allowed back on the decks. There were three cabins on the ship, and because of my husband's acquaintance with the owner of the Phoenix, our families were able to book two of the cabins. Several of the unmarried miners obtained a third cabin. There were about 100 passengers below decks in steerage. There was little privacy, and hammocks were their beds.

The first full day at sea, the waves were pitching and rolling. When we were called to muster, many of the people were sick and retching. Two cooking fires were started, and two lines were formed and we waited our turn to cook. When we neared the coast of Ireland, the weather was so bad, other passengers told us that their belongings were tossing everywhere below decks if it wasn't tied down. That night, the winds had ceased and the sea had calmed. There were several musicians on board. They started playing and those who had recovered from seasickness began dancing and singing.

As the days turned into weeks, the people in steerage continued to get sick, due to the constant tossing of the ship. It rained a lot and the water would seep below decks, and making it very damp and cold. The decks became increasingly slippery. During the days of stormy weather, the passengers were forced to stay down below. It was dark and damp there, with no light except for when the hatches were opened. There was always a danger of fire because the only means of light would be candles and the passengers had to be very careful. Everything below got wet during these bad weather days – the bedding, the clothes, even the crated food. When the weather finally broke, we had a good sunny day, but it was very windy. The crew was ordered to clean out the steerage, as it was beginning to smell. The families had to move all their belonging above to the main deck. If they did not lash everything down, it was blown away.

After we had been traveling for several weeks, the crew put empty casks on the main deck. After we had many days of rain, the casks were full of water. The water was warmed by the sun and this enabled us to take turns getting baths after stormy weather. As for the daily call of nature, we had to use buckets (and some people brought their chamber pots). Ropes were tied to the handles and they were thrown overboard and rinsed out with seawater.

What did we do for entertainment? When we had good weather, we were all allowed on the main deck. I liked to read my Bible, and I had brought a few other books that we shared and swapped with others. A preacher was on board. So we were able to have Bible study and hear sermons and sang hymns. Some people played whist, or other card games.. Others kept journals of their journey. Several passengers brought musical instruments.

On days when the sea was choppy, the seamen called the waves "white sheep". Everyone was drenched when a wave came over and washed the deck. We had to go to change clothes, and we were getting tired of the salty air and spray. On many occasions, we saw porpoises racing with the ship and areas with whales.

William told me the ship averaged 10 knots on good days. The men carried muskets and guns in the event we needed protection from pirates. This was never a problem. There were some days when there was no wind. On one calm day, the Captain set out his small boat and invited those men who had rifles to come along and shoot at a flock of birds that happened to cross our path. On another windless day, William *and the boys went fishing with a few men and caught many cod. We enjoyed a fish fry that night.*

As we neared America, we sailed into a dreadful storm; the Phoenix was tossed and hit by large waves. We lost a mast. I thought we were going to drown. The crew had to tie themselves to the rigging so they would not fall overboard. William had gone below decks to help out, because many of the people were sick with small pox. Several people had already died from this disease. William and your brother, Robert, became sick with small pox; William was ailing when we arrived in Baltimore and he died in Richmond. Robert survived, but the disease left pock marks on his face.

I was widowed with five children, in an unknown country. My brother John and his friend, Richard Lewis, assisted us during this overwhelming time for me. I considered my options and decided to stay in Virginia with my family. Richard offered companionship and support during my husband's illness and death. Even though I was several years his senior and had children, he asked for my hand in matrimony one year after William's death. Your children may have questions about their heritage. I hope this information will be passed down through the generations.

With all my love,

Momma.

Chapter 6 ~Thomas Newell's Letter 1810~

As much as I did not want to admit it, I was very curious about the history of our family. To think that Anne's family settled right here in this area and that Rose actually lived in the house that Anne's brother, Thomas, built over 200 years ago!

After a fitful night's sleep, I arose the next morning, ready to read another journal. As usual, I met Mom in the kitchen, who was toasting some bagels. "Good morning, Mom. It looks like I came down at the right time, as I grabbed a mug and poured some coffee."

Mom replied, "Yes, it's a lovely morning. Would you like to join me in the sunroom with a bagel?"

"Sure," I said as I followed her to the table. "I finished the letter from Anne last night. I'm ready to read another one."

"Well let's have a look in the Hannah Box and pick out two more." Mom shuffled through the papers. She handed me a large, folded parchment. "Would you like to read this one next?"

"Sounds good to me," as I gently grasped the paper from Mom's hand. I unfolded the long sheet of paper, a small envelope slid out on the table. I ignored it for the moment; focusing my attention on the document. The ink was still legible on the calligraphy script. "It looks like a will, Mom.

"It must be Thomas Newell's will. He left his estate to Anne's children." Moms picked up the smaller envelope and opened it. "Let's see what this says," as she began to read the letter.

Dec 5, 1810

My Dearest Anne,

I recently received a letter from Timothy Sutton. In an attempt to do the proper thing, he crafted a spar box for me. He enclosed a key with this letter and asked me to return to England and reclaim my bequest.

I am confiding in you about the money in the event that I am not able to return to England to visit Timothy, accept his gift and my inheritance. The letter with the key is in my strongbox. I am leaving my estate to your children, maybe one of my nephews will be able to visit our homeland and retrieve the money before the location of this spar box is lost.

I remain, your loving brother,

Thomas

"Mom, do you know anything about the key and this inheritance?" I asked.

"No, I don't," she pondered, "I wonder if Rose might have some ideas. Why don't you take this letter over to her?"

"That's a great suggestion!" I responded. "This is getting exciting. Maybe there is some long lost money waiting for Uncle Thomas' relatives!" I finished my coffee, got the car keys from Mom and drove over to visit Rose again.

Chapter 7~ Thomas Newell 1793 ~

My brother, John, and I are in partnership with the miners at the Dufton Fell lead mines just behind the village of Dufton. I am a blacksmith and toolmaker, and John manages the maintenance at the mines. Richard Lewis runs the smelting furnace for the surrounding mines. Though Richard is several years younger, but we have been friends for years.

Having been devout Roman Catholics in their younger years, my family attended St. Cuthbert's church in the adjacent village of Knock, and the Lewis' attended The Church of St. Margaret and St. James in their village of Long Marton. More recently, John and I have strayed from the conformity of our religion. When we were children, our father took us with him on a visit to the Watson mines on business. On our way to lunch at the neighboring village of Alston, our attention was drawn to a crowd forming at Market Cross, where the Methodist evangelist, John Wesley was preaching. This was his second visit to Alston (the first appearance being in 1748). Although Mr. Wesley did not think he had made an impression in the townsmen made up of Quakers and Catholics, Alston had established one Methodist church prior to Mr. Wesley's second visit in 1770. Methodism intrigued our father and he renewed his commitment to God. As a result, he was instrumental in establishing a Methodist church in Dufton.

Gatherings were usually at church, and the miners usually attended to get a rest from working long days during the week at the mines. At one of these church picnics, I met Sally Graves. Our families lived in the same village. She was just 18 and I had just turned 31. I know there was a great age difference, but I was quite taken with her beauty. She was a sister to Robert and Joseph Graves. Both brothers worked at Park Hill Mine where I was the mine smith. Sally and I would take long walks across Dufton Fell. We shared the same love of nature.

One day, after having dinner with Sally and her family, we excused ourselves and started down the path toward the fell. "Sally," I began," I have some interesting news. A business partner of mine returned from America recently. There is a mining company in Virginia that is looking for men from our area experienced in mining operations. I was thinking about traveling over there.

Sally turned to me and responded, "Well, you know the trade well. When would you return?"

We stopped walking and facing her, I clasped her hands, "I was thinking about moving there and I want you to come with me. I have already spoken to your father to ask for your hand in marriage. Would you marry me?"

Sally looked me in the eyes, "I love you very much, but I don't think I could leave my family; I'll have to ponder about this. When would you be leaving?"

"My plan is to leave at the beginning of Spring".

Sally replied, "That is only six months away!"

"When you talked to my father, did he know you were considering about going to America?"

"No, I wanted to get his permission to marry you first. Then I wanted to discuss it with you. If you agree to marry me, then we could discuss it with your father together, "I responded. "Contemplate about it, and we will discuss it after the New Year." We walked back to the house, said our good-byes and went home.

That night, I conferred with my brother, John, about the situation. He reminded me that her brothers were very protective of her and thought they would persuade her to stay in England. I saved some money and along with the inheritance I received from my uncle; all I had to do was investigate a suitable vessel for passage to America after the winter weather had subsided. John was agreeable with my pursuit of lead mining in Virginia. He said that if it was prosperous that he would consider moving as well.

The holidays came and went, and before I knew it, it was January 1st, 1793. Sally and I were going to market. I helped her into the buggy. As we rode to town we began to discuss the inevitable. I spoke first, "Sally, I've given you several months to think about my proposal, will you marry me and accompany me to America?"

Sally smiled and looked at me with her beautiful blue eyes and answered, "I've given it a lot of thought," she threw her arms around my neck and said, "Yes I'll marry you and go with you to America!"

I released her grasp and asked her, "Does your family have this same sentiment?"

"I talked it over with mother and father. Father knows you will be a good husband." She continued, "Mother took it hard, me being her only daughter, but she wants me to be happy."

I asked her, "What about your brothers?"

"Robert and Peter have hard heads. They don't want me to leave. They think it will make Mother grieve, as if I had died. But I don't care what they think, since Father has given his blessing."

This was the happiest day of my life. We talked and made plans about our future. Later that evening, I decided to celebrate by visiting the local pub in the village. I knew a lot of the miners would be there and I had something to brag about. I sat down with some miners, Timothy and Edward Sutton who were brothers. We drank several pints of ale. I guess I drank a little too much. I told my friends that I had been offered a job in Virginia and that I had finally found a use for my inheritance. Sally's brothers came over to our table as they heard me proudly announce to my friends of my upcoming marriage to Sally and journey to America. Robert and Joseph were very upset about Sally's decision. I told them it was none of their concern, as Mr. Graves had given his blessing. The argument turned from a shouting match to a brawl. Several customers got involved in the squabble and I left the pub before I did anything that I would later regret. Thankfully, I managed to saunter home and tumbled into bed.

Upon returning home on Monday evening from the Watson Mine, I noticed a horse tied up to the post in the front yard. Constable Eric Wood was sitting on my front step, "Good evening, Thomas, may I have a word with you?" he said as he arose to shake my hand.

"Good evening, Eric, won't you come inside for a cup of tea," as I unlocked the door and escorted him into the parlor. Eric's family and my family lived in the same village.

"I'll pass on the tea, Thomas," as he sat down, "Where were you today."

I sat down across from him, "I've been at Watson, why do you ask?"

"Thomas, there has been an accident at the Park Hill Mine. Four miners were killed."

I asked, "Who?'

"Sally Graves' brothers, Robert and Joseph, and their cousins, Michael and Nathan Patterson," the Constable replied. "Thomas, the miners all know that you had an argument with Sally's brother over your engagement' The Chief Constable has reason to believe you were responsible for the accident."

"What? You think I deliberately created a mining accident to kill Sally's brothers?"

"Thomas, I'm sorry, you are under investigation and I'm asking you as a friend, to remain in the village for a while."

"Certainly, Eric."

Eric rose to leave, "Thanks Thomas," he said as he shook his hand, "I don't believe that you are responsible; I hope we can prove it."

I escorted Eric to the door and watched him walk down the path to his horse. I couldn't believe what I had heard. Word would spread throughout the villages about the accident and people would believe that I was responsible for my friend's deaths. I had to do some quick thinking. I knew that Sally would not leave her parents now. If I left for America as soon as I could book passage, then I would be free from prosecution. I must leave for Liverpool tomorrow, no tonight. I gathered my belongings together and reached under my bed and pulled out my box that contained most of my inheritance from my uncle. It seemed too easy to pull out from under my bed. I opened it and the coins were gone! Who could have taken them? I had planned on using that money to get settled in America. What was I to do now?

Fortunately, I had enough money saved up from my wages, enough to purchase a ticket, but it was in the bank in Appleby. I could not ask my brother for a loan, because I didn't want anyone to know I was leaving. I quickly penned a note to Sally, assuring her that I was not responsible for the deaths of her brothers. I told her that I loved her and that I regretted having to depart without her. I also left a note for my brother, explaining the situation, asked him to give Sally her note, and told him I would send word to him after I was settled in America. After gathering my belongings, I waited until dawn, saddled my horse and rode to Appleby which was only one hour's ride away.

I withdrew my savings from the bank and headed for Liverpool. The authorities would not realize I was gone for at least twenty-four hours, and I would be in Liverpool long before they began their search.

When I arrived in Liverpool, I found a merchant vessel that was departing from port the following day, bound for Baltimore, Maryland. The Captain and I agreed on a fare. I sold my horse, enabling me to have enough funds to secure means of transportation when I arrived in Baltimore. Thus began a new chapter in my life.

Chapter 8 ~Timothy Sutton, 1810~

My older brother, Edward and I had been friends with Thomas and John Newell since childhood. In fact, we were actually distant cousins. We shared the same features – dark curly hair, and hazel eyes. Our grandmothers were sisters. Thomas' grandfather, Roger, was a wealthy landowner. His great-uncle Randall a prosperous partner of a merchant shipping company, left his fortune to his nephew, who in turn bequeathed it to his sons, Thomas and John. The Newells employed my grandfather, Alexander Sutton who maintained their financial records.

Roger Newell had two sons, Roger Dalton (called Dalton to distinguish him from his father) and John, father of my friends, Thomas and John (Junior). Mr. Newell retained a tutor for their children. Our family lived in a cottage on the Newell land and because we were close in age to the Newell children, Mr. Newell allowed my brother and me to learn to read and write with his children. Edward always thought of us as the poor relations, but I never felt that way. I remain forever thankful to Mr. Newell for affording me the opportunity of education.

Edward, on the other hand, hated every minute of schooling. We were as different as night and day. He wasn't interested in learning, and constantly getting into trouble. Edward's earliest shenanigans began when he was about seven years old. He came to lessons early one morning and placed a handful of cockleburs under the saddle blanket of our tutor's horse. After lessons were over, Edward whispered in my ear to look out the window and watch our teacher leave. As he put his foot into the stirrup, his horse would not sit still. As he swung his leg over and before he settled into his seat, his horse started bucking and threw him off his back. Mr. Newell had been standing on the porch steps and ran down to help him up. Edward was laughing, but I didn't think it was funny. Thomas's sister, Anne, was peeking into the doorway and saw Edward. She ran out of the house and whispered something to her father. Mr. Newell helped our tutor up and they inspected his steed's saddle blanket and found the cockleburs. I learned later that Anne observed Edward earlier from her bedroom window before lessons. She was not certain what he was doing to the horse, but when she saw him laughing, she realized that he was not just petting the horse.

Then there was the time that Edward loosened the axel pin in a wheel of the straw cart that I was driving. I had almost gotten to the barn when the cart wheel fell off and all the straw toppled out of the cart. It was late in the day and I had to find another axel pin, repair the wheel, reload the straw and get it into the barn before nightfall. I cannot fathom the reason for Edward's meanness.

Mr. Newell had graciously deeded the cottage and the small plot of land, to our parents, since they had worked for him for so many years. Edward and I continued to live there as well, since we knew our father would pass the home place to us one day. We went to work as miners. We were very fortunate to live close enough to the mines to walk to and from work daily. Many of our friends lived the five work days a week at the mining shop and then went home on the weekends. The mining shop consisted of small rooms with bunks and a small kitchen. About 16 men lived together in these rooms. It was difficult for me to live in a cottage with Edward, let alone a room full of men.

There were two parishes near Dufton, depending on where one lived. We lived closer to St. Cuthbert's parish. The Newell and Sutton families attended church services every Sunday. But later I joined the Methodist church that Mr. Newell had funded and built, due to the preaching of Reverend John Wesley. Protestantism made much more sense to me, it was more personal, and did not place so much emphasis on rituals. Of course, Edward stopped going to church all together as soon as he had the chance. By the grace of God, we made it through our younger years to adulthood without any major catastrophes... until the mining accident.

At the end of the work week, many of us would go to the local pub and have a few drinks, talk and play cards. On one of these nights, Thomas had informed us that he was going to marry Sally Graves and go to America as a mining supervisor. He boasted about the money that he had inherited. Sally's brothers were not happy about this engagement. Thomas had too much to drink and told her brothers that nothing would stop him from carrying out his plan, not even them. Unfortunately, Edward was a very greedy soul. He and one of his friends devised a plan to steal the money from Thomas, and sabotage one of the mining shafts. Several men were killed. Of course, Thomas was the prime suspect and he left for America as soon as he had found out about the incident. I grieved for Sally and her parents.

In a drunken stupor, Edward came home that night and told me everything and threatened to kill me if I went to the authorities. He had bullied me all my life and I chose to remain silent. Edward knew he had to wait until the investigation was completed before he could profit from the gold coins. One night, I secretly followed Edward out to the barn and saw him bury the strongbox. After waiting several hours, I then dug up the strongbox and hid it myself. I could not surmise how I was going to do it, but I was going to try my best to get Thomas' inheritance back to him. When Edward realized that the strongbox had been removed, he was belligerent. Of course, he couldn't report the "theft". This discovery ultimately resulted in Edward's death. He lost his job, drank all the time and apparently walked away from the pub one night and fell off an escarpment.

With Edward gone, I thought my life would get easier. Though I loved my brother, I was glad to be free from the torment. I had time to think about how to return Thomas' bequest. Many of the miners handcrafted boxes and used the colorful quartz and feldspar stones to make beautiful scenes in these boxes. I started collecting these stones and constructed a spar box of my own. I had the idea of inserting a secret compartment in the bottom of the box to hide the coins.

Before I completely finished the spar box, I had a fall while working, crushing the bones in my leg. The mining company transported me to a hospital in Appleby where I stayed for weeks until I was able to walk on a crutch. My life as a miner had ended and I did not know how I was going to continue making a living. There was no other substantial employment in Dufton. The owners of most of the local mines were Quakers and, fortunately, as compensation for my permanent injury, let me stay in one of their rooms in a local inn. There I met a kindly old gentleman, Mr. Horace Brantley. He was an accountant for a bank in Appleby and was retiring soon. We became friends and talked in the study many nights, and shared stories about our lives. When I told Mr. Brantley about my education and being adept with numbers, he took me to meet the bank president the next day. Thanks be to God, that I was hired to replace Mr. Brantley's position when he retired.

During this time, I pondered my options of returning the money to Thomas. I did not want to lose my job, so taking a voyage to America was out of the question. Thomas's friend and business associate, Richard Lewis, traveled to and from America several times a year as he had business ventures in both countries. I knew that Thomas trusted Richard. I thought about giving him Thomas' bequest to return to him; but that just would not work. Too many complications could arise. We have a local mail service, the London Two Penny Post, and a new foreign office had been opened to deliver and receive posts from abroad; but this was not always reliable, especially since I did not know where to address the letter. The spar box was still at the cottage. I had been away from home for several months. Mr. Brantley let me borrow a carriage so I could return home for a weekend. One of Mr. Newell's caretakers had been tending to the cottage during my absence. I was working on my spar box that evening and the solution came to me. I removed the lock mechanism from an old door Next I bored a hole and carved a slot into the drawer, thus fastening it on the inside. When the door key was inserted to this specific opening at the bottom of the spar box, the secret drawer would open where I had placed the coins. I decided to pen a letter to Thomas, wrap the letter around the key, and place it in an envelope. The next time Richard was in the area, I planned to give the letter to him, addressed to Thomas, and ask him to present it to him upon his arrival back to America. I knew that this would ensure that

64

Thomas would receive my letter. I moved the spar box and its secret contents to the cellar and put a padlock on the door. It was too heavy for me to transport back to Appleby and I felt it would be safer in the cellar. If I was still in Appleby when Thomas returned, the Newells could get word to me and I would gladly meet him at the cottage.

After a few months, I managed to move out of the Inn, eternally grateful to the mining company. I rented a room in a boarding house in Appleby. I no longer needed to use a crutch, but walked with a slight limp. Appleby was a quaint, little town, within riding distance from Dufton. The Eden River ambled alongside the main venue. It was home to the Appleby Castle and St. Lawrence Church. The main street, Boroughgate, was very wide and was lined with various shops that housed various businesses. It was home to St. Lawrence Church to the north end and Appleby Castle to the south end. As part of my recuperation, I strolled up and down the street and I began to meet folks at the weekly market that was always set up on the square. Farmers set up booths with fresh produce and others that offered anything from local honey, handicrafts, fresh flowers, soaps, candles and baked goods. The first time I ventured to the weekly market, I spotted the books, my favorite booth. As I reached for a tome, I heard the sweetest voice, "May I help you, sir?"

Startled, I looked up and my gaze fell upon the face of an angel. She had long, auburn hair that toppled over her shoulders like a waterfall. Her eyes were sparkling green and she had freckles dotted over her nose and cheeks. She was slim and wore a blue frock with a white apron. She smiled sweetly, as she awaited my reply. "I… I was looking a this volume, " I stammered looking blankly at the book.

"Ah, you like Jonathan Swift. Gulliver's Travels is an excellent choice! Have you read his other works?"

I answered meekly, "Well, I have read some of his poems and short stories, Miss…,"

She replied, "My name is Rachel, Miss Rachel Lindsey."

"Timothy Sutton, I have been recuperating in Appleby after injuring my leg."

"I surmise that you have some leisure time for reading. My I recommend this book to you?"

I checked my pocket to see if I had any shillings. "Yes, Miss Lindsey, I would like to purchase this book". We continued to chat for a little while and I bade her good day and returned with a livelier step to my room.

Chapter 9 ~Timothy Sutton's ~Letter 1810

I drove to Rose's house and practically ran to the front door. I rang the doorbell and impatiently waited for her to open the door, nervously tapping my foot. After a few seconds, Rose opened the door and invited me to come in. I relayed the events of this morning to her as we walked back to her kitchen. Rose poured two cups of coffee for us and we sat down. I handed her the letter and after she had finished perusing it, I asked, "Do you know anything about this strongbox?"

Rose thought for a moment. "I have quite a collection of things that my family has saved through the years. Let's go see if we can find this strongbox". Rose got up from the table and I followed her up the stairs to her bed room and through what looked like a closet door. It turned out to be the entrance to her attic. The room was in immaculate order, with shelves of boxes that were numbered. Rose picked up a notebook from the first shelf. "Let's see," as she opened the notebook. She ran her fingers down the pages. "Shelf 8, box number 5". I was amazed at her organization. We walked over to the designated spot. "That one," as she pointed to the appropriate box, "could you be a dear and get it down for me?"

"Gladly," I answered as I stood on my tiptoes, grabbed the box and set it on the floor. Rose opened the box and shuffled her hands inside it. "Here it is, "as she grabbed its handle and pulled it out of its resting place. She turned to me and said, "Why don't we take it down to the kitchen where the light is better?" I don't know who was more anxious, Rose, or me, as we trotted down the stairs toward the kitchen.

Rose set the strongbox on the table. "Let's see what is inside," she said as she opened the latch. There were various articles of memorabilia including a pocket watch, a pair of eyeglasses, and some Confederate money. At the bottom of the box was an old, yellowed, envelope addressed to Thomas Newell, Rural Retreat, Virginia. Rose handed it to me, "Will you read it for me? I left my reading glasses upstairs in my bedroom."

There was an indentation in the paper on the front. I carefully slipped my finger under the flap. I pulled out the letter and unfolded it. An object dropped to the table. "This must be the key that Thomas mentioned in his letter to Anne!" I began reading the letter.

July 10, 1810

Dear Thomas,

With a heavy heart I write to you. For many years I have been carrying a momentous burden. With this letter, I intend to confess the truth and reveal a deeply buried past. It has been nearly five years since that fateful night at the pub. That insignificant brawl between you and the Graves brothers over Sally led to disaster. I know that you were falsely accused of the deaths of Robert and Joseph Graves, and their cousins, Michael and Nathan Patterson.

My confession begins with the criminals that stole your gold coins. It was Edward and Nathan; they knew you had the gold coins because you announced it in a drunken proclamation. I realize you must be furious with me right now and for that I am deeply sorry. You have probably figured it out by now, but I wanted to tell you that Edward and Nathan stole your gold coins. Later that night, Nathan Patterson came by our house. I had already gone to bed, but I could hear Nathan and Edward contriving a plan. Nathan shared with Edward that you must have saved up a lot of money to travel to America, and by then he convinced Edward to steal into your home. While you were at church that Sunday, they agreed find to the coins. I tried to reason with Edward, but he would not hear of it. Nathan and Edward sneaked into your house, and searched until they found the box of coins tucked away beneath your bed. Edward hid the money and told me where it was, for he had a lack of trust in Nathan's word. Edward must have been consumed with greed, for he told me that he wished to kill Nathan and make it look like a mining accident. I convinced myself that Edward spoke these words because he was inebriated.

Tragically, we found out that not only Nathan, but his brother and the Graves brothers were all killed in a cave at

Park Hill Mine. Edward knew that you would be prime suspect in the accident because of the threats you made at the pub; but Edward was responsible. He weakened the struts in the new vertical shaft of the mine, which resulted in the cave-in. You and I both know Edward has always had a bad temperament. I am ashamed to confess that I never saw this vile nature. Edward threatened to kill me if I ever went to the authorities. As a consolation, he said he would share your money with me I daresay, I had no choice.

I am deeply sorry. I beg you to read on to know more about this heinous crime. I know you had no choice but to flee to America and save yourself from arrest. In time, Edward revealed his plans; he was going to hide the money away for a while until all suspicions rested. Then one night, Edward left the house with your money in a box. I followed him and watched him bury the box. Before he finished burying it, I quietly departed to the house. He never knew I followed him. As time progressed, I made my move. Edward went to market one day, and I ran out to the field, dug out the money box, threw the money in a bag, and re-hid the money in our barn. About a year passed, and Edward dug up the box and found the money was gone. Needless to say, he was infuriated and told me that the money was gone. He never suspected that I was the culprit. Under the circumstances, he could not report it missing.

Edward became obsessed about the money taken from the buried box. He could only talk to me about the loss of the coins. Edward frequented the pub nightly and would come home quite drunk. One morning I awoke to find that my brother's bed had not been slept in and he was nowhere to be found. Later that day, the constable came to our home to tell us they had found Edward's body at the bottom of an escarpment. Only God knows what happened. The authorities determined his death accidental; they thought he must have left the tavern and wandered across the moor to the escarpment at Dufton Fell. It was a petty, selfish, and greedy act that forced you to flee to the Americas I have kept this secret for many years, for fear of my own murder at my brother's hands.

Guilt has consumed my thoughts about what happened. I want to repay you for the heartache you must have felt, in an attempt make up for what Edward did. I actually borrowed the idea from a natural scientist, Sir David Brewster, from Edinburgh. Sir David was visiting distant relatives in Durham and he was asked to speak at the town square about his new invention, a kaleidoscope. He had developed a type of toy that looked like a small telescope. Inside it were colorful beads and glass chards that were set inside the tip of the tube of the telescope. There was an eyepiece at one end of the tube, and between the eyepiece and the bead and chards of glass was a set of mirrors. The end of the tube could be turned and when it was pointed up toward light, as the end of the cylinder rotated, *because of the mirrors, the beads and pebbles made different designs with each turn of the cylinder.*

Not long after that, I was injured, and was no longer able to work in the mines. Before the accident, our mining crew found several cavities that were lined with beautiful crystals. We collected many minerals and quartz of an array of colors in the veins. My fascination with the kaleidoscope led me to fashion an image of similar shapes and colors of minerals that were held together with glue. Having a collection of various colors of quartz from the gangue, I glued together pieces of bonny bits to form a rock picture. In the center is a white, quartz cross, surrounded with yellow copper. The cross is outlined with tiny pieces of zinc ore. I had a single piece of red fluorspar and placed it in the center of the cross. The background is an assortment of fluorspar, forming a sky of blue and green. The ground is brownish yellow. By one of the old entrances to the mineshaft, I found some lengths of wood, the breath of each measuring about one foot. I fashioned a frame with elaborate fretwork from these pieces. The framed mineral picture was then placed in a wooden box that was nearly the size of a cabinet, measuring three by four feet. The scene is in the center of the box. I set a mirror on each side of the frame to enhance the image. Additionally, candles can be placed in the lower corners of the box to illuminate the shiny minerals and reflect the color with the mirrors. Behind the fretwork on the bottom of the cabinet is a hidden drawer. I secured the corners of the fretwork with two wooden pegs, to hide the fact that the fretwork hides the front face of the drawer. There is a key to unlock the hidden drawer.

Begging for forgiveness, I made you this gift and I wish to return what is rightfully yours. Enclosed in this letter is the key to the drawer. I am sending this to you in case I meet my Maker before you are able to return to England. You see, inside that drawer are all of your coins. If I am not around when you come to pick up your peace-offering, remember that you have to remove the two wooden pegs from the fretwork. This allows this strip of trim to flip up and reveal the hidden drawer.

It is my hope that you reply to my letter before long. I eagerly await our reunion and the coins returned to their rightful owner.

Most respectfully yours,

Timothy Sutton

"Obviously Thomas did not go back to England before he died", I said.

Rose added, "I wonder if that spar box still exists, and if it does, I wonder, where is it? This letter was written over 155 years ago!"

"Rose, where do we start looking for the spar box?" I asked.

Rose thought for a moment. "Let's ask your mom, she is the genealogy nut."

Chapter 10 ~What is a Spar Box?~

I returned home to find a note left by my Mom on the kitchen table stating she and Dad had gone to town to buy groceries. I couldn't wait for Mom to get back so I grabbed my laptop and googled spar boxes and found three web pages. All of them confirmed that the Mining Heritage in Killhope, in Northern England had the National Collection of Spar Boxes. They were made by lead miners, were various shapes and sizes, and were also called spar cases or spar columns. There were several photographs depicting several varieties, from small and simple construction, to large, ornate structures. Next, I searched for Killhope Museum. Their webpage gave way to an exhibition of 24 spar boxes. Killhope Mining Museum was in Upper Weardale, County of Durham, England. The word, spar, is from the word fluorspar, and is one of the minerals found in the lead mines. Apparently the construction of spar boxes was a local art among miners, only indigenous to the area of the Northern Pennines of England, and only around the 1800s and dying out in the early 1900s, when much of the lead mining ended.

I was finishing perusing an article on spar boxes when Mom and Dad came in the front door with hands full of grocery bags. I jumped up from my stool at the kitchen counter and ran to them. "Mom, you won't believe it! Rose found the strongbox in her attic that Thomas wrote about to his sister! The letter from his friend and the key were in the box! Thomas apparently never made it back to England to obtain his money. Mom, how far is Weardale from Dufton? "

As Mom and Dad were setting the groceries on the table, Mom said, "My goodness! We leave for a few minutes and look at what we miss! Let me finish putting away the groceries and we'll take a look." Luckily, Dad said that he would finish putting away the stuff, so Mom and I made our way to the computer. It turned out that Weardale was in the County Durham (Americans switch the wording around and would say Durham County), is next door to County Cumbria. She ascertained that there was about 15 miles between Dufton and Weardale, as a crow flies, but within an hour's driving distance.

I was so excited that I couldn't contain myself. I had not started looking for a summer job, so wondered what Mom and Dad would think about going to England. "So Mom, since you and Dad planned to spend the rest of the summer here, whaddya say we take a side trip to jolly ole England?"

Mom thought about the idea for a moment and said, "Well, I have always wanted to visit England, especially since we know the villages where our ancestors used to live. I'll have to talk to your father about it after lunch." That was enough for me. Dad liked to plan spur-of-the-moment adventures. Because Mom and Dad took cruises several times a year, they had current passports and my passport was less than a year old, having recently returned from Italy for a few course credits last year.

Austin came in for lunch and I caught him up with Rose's and my latest discovery. I explained that it looked like we were going to England and asked him if he wanted to go with us. He said that he would have to stay behind and tend to the farm and stay close to home in case Rose needed him for something. I was a bit relieved that he didn't want to go. He didn't have a passport and the summer would be over if we waited for him to get one.

After lunch, I walked out on the back porch and sat in the swing sipping some tea and leafing through a magazine, patiently waiting for my parents' decision. Time seemed to drag by, and finally, Mom and Dad step outside and joined me on the porch. Dad spoke first, "Aspen, Mom and I have been talking about going to England. Since we hadn't decided what we were going do to for your graduation from college, we have decided that a trip to England would be an early graduation present."

I jumped up and hugged Dad around the neck, "Oh thank you!, I think that is a great idea! When do we leave?"

"I'll have to call our travel agent and see how quickly he can arrange a flight and accommodations for us. Your mother has given me a list of places where she wants to visit. I'll let you know as soon as I know something."

"I'll check and see what the temperatures are there now." We always packed an abundance of clothing. The weather in this part of southwest Virginia was very similar to that in northeast Georgia this time of year. It turned out that the weather in England was a little cooler, but there was a tendency for more rain than we are accustomed.

The next day, Dad reported that our travel agent was able to book a flight out of Richmond on Thursday (two days away). We would transfer in New York and by Friday, we would arrive in Edinburgh, Scotland. That gave us time to shop for the extra items for the excursion.

Chapter 11 ~Timothy and Rachel's Courtship~

I had never been happier in all my life. Six months into my employment, I was advanced to the position of a loan officer which afforded me an increase in my wages. I was still living at the boarding house, my expenses were few and I put back money every week from my earnings into a savings account. My friendship with Rachel had developed into a courtship. After that first visit to the market, I increased my reading habits so I could return to Rachel's table to purchase another book. Over a course of several months, I read many books. One of my favorite authors (and Rachel's as well) was Daniel Defoe. His book, Robinson Crusoe, was actually based on actual events of a mariner marooned on an island. He later penned, The Further Adventures of Robinson Crusoe, and Serious Reflections During the Life and Surprising Adventures of Robinson Crusoe. I also read books by Matthew Gregory Lewis and Horace Walpole.

After several months had transpired, I drew the courage to ask Rachel to attend the Appleby Horse Fair. This event has been taking place since 1685, for a week in June, on Fair Hill, just outside Appleby. It attracts horse traders from all around the country, especially gypsies and Romany families. Rachel agreed to accompany me. We decided to go to the fair on Saturday, as this was the day that the races would take place on Flashing Lane.

Rachel lived at home with her parents. They did not live far from Boroughgate. Her father, Trevor, was a bookseller as well as a librarian. They lived in a small, two story abode with the yard was lined with several beds of flowers. Her mother, Emily, tended the immaculate garden that was filled with roses of various colors. As I arrived at her doorstep, Rachel must have been looking out her window, because she opened the door before I had a chance to knock, and handed me a large picnic basket and a blanket. She stepped out the door with her parasol in hand. "Hello Timothy, I have anxiously awaited this day!" she exclaimed. Normally, Rachel was very shy whenever I visited her at the market.

"Good day, Rachel," I replied as I tried to tip my hat while managing the blanket and basket. We walked down the street to Boroughgate and found a lovely spot under a huge shade tree and spread out the blanket. We chatted about books, her mother's flower garden, and the lovely weather, and waited for the horse races to begin. Several of our friends settled around the tree as well and we enjoyed a wonderful afternoon.

At the end of the day, we gathered up our things and I found the courage to ask Rachel if I might hold her hand as we walked back home. She did not object. As we neared her home, I wished the moment would not end. I looked into her eyes, now holding both hands, and said, "I had a splendid time today being with you."

"And I as well," she replied.

I knew it was too soon to ask for a kiss, so I just squeezed her hands and bade her good bye. She picked up the empty basket and blanket and turned and walked through the door. "See you tomorrow, I have a new book I want to show you," and she waved goodbye. I smiled in acknowledgement then turned and walked back to my room, reminiscing about the wonderful events of the day.

,

Chapter 12 ~Edinburgh ~

I had never been on a trans-Atlantic flight before. Basically, you fly over the ocean during the night. Thankfully, the jet was one of the bigger ones, with three sections of seats and two aisles. We were in one of the newer jets and there was a movie screen on the back of each seat. There was a selection of movies, so we had our choice of several movies. After the movie was over, the aisle lights were cut off and people started getting comfortable for the night. I started reading a novel. I got tired and tried to get comfortable, but couldn't find a resting position. I also can't sleep with noise (except when falling asleep while watching TV when I'm very tired) so I wear ear plugs while sleeping at night. I brought an eye mask as well. Nothing worked. I couldn't get to sleep. I finished reading my novel, maneuvering my inflatable neck pillow with the little one the airlines provide along with a blanket, and finally dropped off to sleep. I probably wasn't asleep for an hour when the lights came up at about 6 AM and the flight attendant announced they would be serving breakfast soon. Needless to say, when we landed in Edinburgh, I was exhausted.

Dad rented a minivan at the airport. He had never been to the United Kingdom, either, and bought a book about the English driving codes. We didn't make it out of the airport parking lot before Dad had to stop and ask someone how to maneuver out of the airport. Driving on the left side of the road was awkward. The roundabouts were even more confusing. Dad had downloaded the maps for Scotland and England on his GPS. Unfortunately, the dash on the van was sloped and he had to put his hand out the window to get a signal. I really got a giggle out of that. Mom was the navigator and kept telling him where to go with the road map.

We somehow made it to Edinburgh, and found the Holiday Inn, just three miles from the Airport, on Corstorphine Road, next door to the Edinburgh City Zoo. The rooms were small, but not as small as the elevators, or lifts as they are called in the United Kingdom. Only one person could fit in the lift with the luggage, and there was barely enough room for that. Dad took the lift and Mom, and I chose the stairs. At least the room was air conditioned. Instead of having a coffee pot, there was a carafe for making hot water, along with mugs, a variety of tea and neatly-stacked, individual creamers. The sugar packets were long and cylindrical instead of the square packets that I was accustomed to seeing in the States.

After our long night flight, we decided to take a nap, even though it was morning in Edinburgh. We were starved when we awoke later that afternoon. Dad called the Concierge to inquire about restaurants. He advised us that the best dishes were actually at the local pubs. Luckily, there was one across the street from the hotel. We ventured over to check it out. I had a steak and onion pie made of tenderloin steak smothered in brown gravy and there was a pastry crust that topped it. It was a most delicious meal!

Dad had decided to enjoy a relaxing trip, so he had planned an outing. The locals were very friendly and helpful, and we had no problem understanding their beautiful accent. We hopped onboard a local, double-decker, red, transit bus, and our first stop was the Princes Gardens which is a part of the grounds of Edinburgh Castle. The Castle is located on a high hill which overlooks the city. We traversed the walking paths surrounded by a plethora of various, colorful flowers and trees. There were many statues in the garden. The only two that were familiar to me were David Livingstone and Robert Louis Stevenson.

Our next stop was the Royal Mile. This Scottish Mile is sandwiched between the University of Edinburgh and Edinburgh Castle. We hiked up the cobbled street toward Edinburgh Castle, which is a part of Old Town. The Castle is one of the oldest European settlements, dating back to 600 AD. King James III built a loch around the castle. During the 1700s, the water became stagnant and it was drained, and the Princes Gardens below the castle was established. We learned that the Military Tattoo performs annually at the entrance of the Castle in August. The old Parliament of Scotland was housed in along this route back in the turn of the 1700s. Edinburgh's present-day legal system resides on the Royal Mile. The trek down High Street was crowded with tourists; many of these old structures are now shops and taverns. Along this strip are many closes, or small side-streets and courtyards. They are commonly named after a former occupant or trader. My favorite shop was down the road from the Castle, the Tartan Weaving Mill. It was run by a kilt maker and had an exhibition of tartan production. Mom purchased some tartan that represented one of the sides of her family whose origins were in Scotland.

As we walked back down the Royal Mile, we took a short-cut stopping on the hillside and took various pictures of the fabulous architecture below, including the National Gallery of Scotland which was comprised of three buildings. We were happy to find out that entrance to the National Gallery of Scotland was free. I was particularly interested seeing the early Renaissance art by Raphael. There were also exhibits of some of my other favorite artists, including Van Gogh, Cezanne and Rembrandt. After walking through the displays in all three buildings, we were quite tired and found another transit bus with a route back to the hotel.

The next morning I awoke first. I could not sleep because I was so excited because of our journey to Northern England. I sprang out of bed, peeking though the drapes. The sky was a light bluish-gray that mixed with a pale red glow from the rising sun as it peeked out over the mountain range in the distance. At the foothills was a thin line of fog that resembled a wisp of smoke and seeming to separate the mountain from the town below. There was a row of buildings that scattered a glimmer of light from streetlights, shops and homes. Between the hotel and the neighborhood was a large field that reminded me of a moor, only speckled with several lines of trees. A dense fog had settled in and floated under the trees. The view was surreal. I later learned that the meadow was actually a golf course!

Chapter 13~ Northern England~

After a fabulous breakfast, we loaded up the minivan and found the proper highway that crossed into England. As we passed through the towns and villages of Scotland, I was amazed at the string of homes. They were usually two-story structures, with wrought-iron fences separating them. Each yard was full of magnificent flower gardens and perfectly manicured lawns. As we approached England, the townships grew farther apart, turning into pastures. The four-lanes narrowed to two-lanes, and the houses gave way to sheep and cattle. We passed through winding mile after mile through the countryside. The fields were separated by rock walls that were about four feet tall. They must have taken years to build. I did not recall seeing a wooden, or chain-link fence. No fences separated the fields from the road. If it had not been for the power poles, one would have thought we had traveled back in time.

As we neared the border, I couldn't help but think about all the battles that were fought in this area in centuries past, between the Scots and the English. We finally reached the summit where Scotland met England. In the United States, when passing from state to state, a sign welcomes you to that state. Not so in the United Kingdom. Since we were passing from country to country, there was more fanfare. There were two areas in which we could stop and take pictures. There was a large boulder in the middle of the parking lot. On one side the word Scotland was printed, and on the opposite side, England was printed. A perfect Kodak moment (or Nikon moment, in this case)! A snack stand was set up; we purchased ice cream bars. A bagpipe player stood close by. Mom and Dad posed in front of a historical marker, and I snapped a shot.

We climbed back into the minivan and headed toward County Northumberland in the District of Tynedale. The mountainous range reminded me of the rolling hills of Virginia. As we approached Redesdale Valley, the countryside gave way to a very quaint village, and we stopped at the Bay Horse Inn. It was a two-story structure with a bevy of flower beds bordering the building. It was lunch time, so we decided to stop and eat lunch. Indeed, pubs were the place to dine and sample the local beer.

We took a slow ride through the North Pennine Mountains, not far from our final destination of the day. We had reservations in the village of Hexham; it was centrally located between several places I wanted to visit. An hour later, we turned into the driveway of our lodging. To my surprise, we were going to stay in a real castle – Langley Castle!

Dad had no problem securing a parking place. We gathered our luggage and entered the castle through massive double doors. Dad obtained a map of the Castle at the reception desk and scheduled a tour of the castle. Our room was on the top floor in the Greenwich Room. Since castles do not have a lift, we had to hike up three flights of stairs, several times a day. Walking into the room, to the right was a window seat set into the stone wall foyer. Across from this was a sitting room with an overstuffed couch. To the left of the couch was a desk with magazines and pamphlets describing local information and attractions. Past the den a door separated the sleeping quarters. This room contained a king-sized, four-poster bed. We ducked through the hallway to the bathroom; the clearance was about five feet.

After settling into our quarters, we journeyed down the stairs to begin our tour. Besides reception, the mail floor hosted the medieval dining room. The guide told us that the castle was built in 1350. Ownership passed between various families through the generations. In the 17th century, it was owned by the Earls of Derwentwater; Viscounts Langley. Charles and James Langley were part of the Jacobite risings in 1715. After imprisonment in the Tower of London, they were executed. The property was acquired by the government. In 1882, it was sold to Cadwallader Bates. He and his wife restored the castle with walls that were seven feet thick.

Between the levels of the main staircase was a remnant of 14th century architecture. Three garderobes sat on the first platform between the first and second story. Before indoor plumbing, these little rooms were on the outside wall and were privies that drained into the moat below and some were used for storage. The second floor housed the drawing room consisting of a large fireplace and stained-glass windows. There were several sitting areas with couches and richly upholstered chairs with a color scheme of shades of red and blue. The window treatments were heavy pleaded drapes, with huge cornice boards trimmed in yellow. The walls boasted several medieval tapestries and massive bookshelves. The third floor contained the rooms for lodging.

We climbed to the top of the castle. The winding stairwells did not have much clearance so we all had to duck to get through them. All four corners of the castle were fortifications for the guards to protect the castle. In medieval times, one form of defense was to pour hot oil form large buckets from the top of the fortress. One of the corner fortifications had been turned into a chapel by one of the previous owners. The view from the guard room was very scenic, high above the treetops. Beyond the castle grounds, I viewed the surrounding farmland; houses and animals dotted the terrain.

At the conclusion of the tour, I returned to our room, retrieved my laptop and headed down the three flights of stairs to the lobby. This was the only hot spot for wireless internet. After questioning the concierge, he handed me some brochures from the local mining museums. My mining ancestors lived in several villages. The mines must have been within walking or horseback riding distance, or they resided in miner lodges during the week. Tomorrow we will visit Watson and Killihope attractions.

Chapter 14~ Watson Mining Museum~

We arrived at the Watson Mining Museum when they opened at 10 AM. After Dad purchased the tickets, we immediately entered the mining museum. There were displays depicting the historical periods of mining, which I read with enthusiasm.

During the later years of the 17th century, the London Lead Company obtained the leases of the mining landowner in Alston. In 1743, this Company designed a village in Alston for the miners and their families. They encouraged the miners to have homesteads. The Company provided cottages with small tracts of land, and an affordable rental fee. The village later expanded to include a church and a school. Another alternative for housing were mine shops, provided for miners who lived farther from the area. These facilities could house up to 40 men during work week. Since I was only interested in mining up to 1800, I searched for my parents. My Dad was busy taking photographs.

"Are you just finished, Dad?"

"Almost, we are scheduled to tour the mine in a few minutes," he replied. The mining guide walked to the back door of the building and requested the group follow him.

We walked outside into a courtyard of sorts and entered a building. Here, the guide told us to pick out our "wellies," which were white rubber, almost knee-length boots. We were also given bright red hard hats and a flash light. Then we walked out of that building stopping at the entrance to the mine shaft. I had to stoop down a little to enter and then I realized why we had on boots. We were walking through water! We were led quite a distance through the mine shaft. We gathered in one area and the guide told us to cut off our flash lights. Of course, it was pitch dark down there. The guide said that the early miners only had candles and lanterns with which to see to mine for the iron ore. As we finished the tour, the guide asked if there were any questions. "Do you know anything about spar boxes?" I asked.

"Spar boxes were made from various colored minerals found in the mines. Most of them were made by miners in the Victorian era", the guide replied.

"Do you have any on display here?"

"No, but one of the best collections is at the Killhope Mining Center, " he answered.

"Where is that?"

"It is Upper Weardale, in the adjoining county. I'll give you a pamphlet with directions back at the museum".

"Thanks!" I exclaimed. "Dad, can we go next to Killihope this afternoon?"

Dad said, "Of course, after we stop somewhere for lunch."

Chapter 15~ Whitfield Tavern~

We passed by Whitfield Tavern on our way to Killhope. Dad decided to stop for our meal. It was a quaint place, with a bar in the center of the room. As we entered, we noticed a group of well-dressed men, donned in chinos and polo shirts, engaging in a lively conversation. Several other men perched at the bar who appeared to be locals. To the right of the bar sat a respectable-looking couple. We chose a table near them.

It didn't take long for the group of men to realize we were not from around the area when we ordered our meal. One of the boisterous gents approached us, and introduced himself. "Hello chaps; my name is Nigel Davis, "as he extended his hand to my Dad, "I fancy you are not from these parts."

My Dad returned the handshake and replied, "Hello Nigel, my name is Cecil. This is my wife, Julia, and my daughter, Aspen". My mother extended her hand, and Nigel grasped her hand and kissed it. Nigel was extremely good-looking, with dark wavy hair, probably in his 40s. I, naturally, extended my hand, and he responded, "I am pleased to make your acquaintance," and kissed my hand as well. Nigel then turned to his cronies and said, "These are my friends, Bernard and Trevor, and that quiet chap sitting by the door, is my chauffer, Jimmy." Bernard and Trevor tipped their pints of ale in recognition, and Jimmy rose from his chair and bowed to us. Chatter around the pub stopped for a moment, and then after the introduction, the others returned to their private conversations. Nigel pulled up a chair, "May I join you for a moment?"

"Certainly," replied my father.

Nigel asked us where we were from, were we on holiday, and how long would we be here. Dad explained that Mom and I were tracing our genealogy roots. Nigel explained that he and his friends come to this area every year to hunt for grouse and pheasants. For some reason, Nigel took a liking to us and told the bartender that he would pay for our meal, and anything we wanted to drink. Nigel noticed that Mom and Dad were sampling local ale; he arose from the table and said to them, "I see that your glasses are almost empty; I will tidy them for you. Nigel took their pints, went behind the bar, topped up the glass, and returned them to our table. He went back to the serving area, continuing to dispense beer to his friends, and offered libations to anyone in the room.

When our meal was served, I asked the waitress, "Excuse me, ma'am, but does Nigel own this pub?"

She replied, "No, my husband, the bartender, and I own this establishment. Every year, during hunting season, Nigel rents the bar for the day, he is very generous."

I don't know anything about bird hunting," I said.

The lady replied, "Hunting brings a lot of income to our area. Our newspaper has a story about it. Would you like me to fetch if for you?"

"Yes, if it isn't too much trouble."

"Not at all; I will be right back," she said as she walked over to her desk. She returned a few moments later and handed me the paper.

The interesting article detailed the elements of hunting. This sport boosts the British economy. It supports many jobs and pays for upkeep of the British countryside. The formal events take place on an estate with a head gamekeeper and a shoot captain. After the birds are shot, there are pickers-up with dogs to collect the game. A party of twenty hunters could pay up to $60,00 a day when hunting for pheasant. In grouse hunting, these huntsmen are limited to 300 birds, and generally, the charge is $100 per bird. If a shooting party shows more than 500 birds, it is considered carnage, and not a sport. Normally the fowl are sold to restaurants. This sport in the United Kingdom is reserved for people with a great deal of money, attracting people from Russia, India and the Arab nations.

We finished our meal and prepared to leave. Dad stepped up to the bar where Nigel persisted to bartend. "Thank you so much for your generosity; we enjoyed the meal and your company!"

Nigel motioned him to come closer, "Cecil, I would like to invite you to go grouse hunting with me and my friends tomorrow."

Dad had that deer-in-headlights look and, for a moment, didn't know how to respond. He politely smiled and after several seconds of thought he replied, "I'm honored, Nigel, but my family and I have plans tomorrow". Dad didn't like to hunt or to fish. He told me once that he had hunted for squirrel with his great-uncle as a boy, but that was the extent of it.

Nigel said, "Sir, you don't realize what an offer that you are turning down!"

"I hope that you accept my respectful decline. I know it is an offer of a lifetime, but my family comes first, and I cannot let them down."

"Understood," Nigel replied, "how I wish that I had a family with which to spend my time."

As we walked to the pub's entrance, several patrons uttered," Cheerio!" We waved back, thanking them for their hospitality.

Chapter 16~ Killhope Mining Museum~

The trip to our next destination was without incident. As soon as Dad parked the car, I hopped out, running to the entrance to the Killhope Museum. "You can't get in until I pay for a ticket!" Dad yelled. I stopped at the door and tried to wait patiently for Mom and Dad.

The museum was similar to the one at Watson, except there was a room full of spar boxes on display of all shapes and sizes. Some were elaborate cabinets filled with colorful ores and minerals and others were smaller and looked like a clock case full of rocks. Each display had a description of the box, its' contents, the name of the craftsman, and the year it was made. Dad took photograph of all of them. I looked for a spar box fitting the description of the one that Timothy had made for Thomas, but none met his description.

One of the employees apparently saw my interest in the spar boxes and came to my side. "Hello, my name is Tyler, do you have any questions?" Tyler looked about my age, was tall and had dark hair with the bluest eyes I had ever seen.

"Well, yes, I do, could you tell me where these spar boxes came from?"

Tyler answered, "The one you are standing next to came from the home of the descendents of the creator of this box, the Egglestone family. Most of them are either on loan from a family or donated to a library or church and are on display here for the year."

"How did you get so many here?"

Tyler responded, "Back in 2003, the National Lottery Fund granted our museum 50,000 pounds for renovation of our building, in order to house these 15 spar boxes"

"Are there any other places that display spar boxes?" I inquired.

Tyler continued, "This art is indigenous to this area, though some historians say that they can be found in Bohemia and Russia, the explanation for this being that a few miners immigrated to Europe. The most extensive collection is here. There is one in the Bowes Museum at Bernard Castle and I believe there are several in the Weardale Museum in Ireshopeburn "

"Where are these museums?"

"Here in County Durham. I have pamphlets I can give you, he offered. "May I ask why you are so interested in spar boxes?"

I carefully considered my answer, not wanting to reveal too much. "My ancestors were miners from Appleby and Dufton. A relative recently showed me some letters that were written back in the 1800s. Several of them mention a spar box that was made as a gift. It was never received because my ancestor came to Virginia, and he was unable to return to England." Tyler pondered a moment," I have an uncle who lives over in Appleby, in County Cambria. He is very knowledgeable in lead mining history of the area. Maybe he could help you."

"Wow that would be great!" I exclaimed.

"He is also a falconer, and manages an attraction for visitors.

I had a cockatiel once, and my uncle has some parrots and macaws," I said.

Tyler explained, "It is kind of like having a macaw perch on your arm, only you have to wear these leather gloves because the talons of these hawks and eagles are so sharp. Basically, you go out in a field with the falconer, wearing the glove, and hold a piece of meat out. The bird will swoop down and land on your arm and eat the meat."

"Let me check with my parents, do you have a business card, so I can call you?"

"Sure." Tyler wrote down his name and number on one of the museum pamphlets and handed it to me. "I am off work this weekend. If you and your family decide to go, call me and I'll make arrangements with my uncle. Maybe I can get you a special deal, since you have an interest in talking to him about lead mining and spar boxes!"

I thanked Tyler for his assistance and went to find my parents who were sitting in the cafe, eating goat cheese and tomato sandwiches. I ordered one myself and sat down to discuss the recent events with them. Naturally, we decided to try our hand at falconry, and get to know Tyler better.

Chapter 17~ Durham Falconry Center~

To my delight, Tyler met us at the Durham Falconry Center at 10 AM on Saturday. We parked and Tyler joined us at our car, and I formally introduced him to my parents. Tyler said, "I think you will find my uncle a world of knowledge, both in the birds and in lead mining." He led us through the entrance to the main grounds, and the mews with various fowl tethered to posts. Many of the birds sat on their perch. There were several smaller barn-like buildings. Tyler explained that the birds perched here during the day and in the evening; they were taken over to barn-like buildings where they roosted at night.

Tyler led us to another structure and as he entered, he called to his uncle. Allen Dent met him at the door. He was a tall, slender, be-speckled man, with thick, white hair, and a white beard, cropped short and neatly trimmed. "Uncle, may I introduce the Blairs to you, all the way from Georgia, in the States. This is Aspen, and her parents, Julia and Cecil."

"A pleasure to meet all of you," Allen warmly replied, as we exchanged handshakes.

"Quite impressive," my father said, "Do you run this by yourself?"

"I have a veterinarian and several part-time people to help me feed and groom the birds, "Allen replied. Allen directed us to a shady area with a picnic table and some chairs. "May I offer you some tea, before we begin?" We politely obliged, sitting down around the picnic table. Allen brought out some tea and biscuits from the closest building and we chatted for a few minutes, while his staff prepared the birds. Allen explained that he was employed as a miner in his youth; he later joined the Royal Air Force. Since retirement, he purchased some birds and opened this establishment.

Part of Allen's introduction to Falconry included a history of the sport. It originated over 4000 years ago in the Far East. This pastime popularized in Medieval Britain as a result of the Norman Conquest. It originally was a means to put food on the table, but eventually changed to a sport of the nobility until the invention of the gun. Falconry was a hobby of the nobility who entertain guests. Castle owners retained a mews and falconer on the grounds.

Before hiking into the pasture, Allen explained that we would take turns wearing the thick, leather glove. Allen carried a knapsack full of raw meat. He described how to put the meat between the gloved thumb and forefinger. The birds would fly to us, and perch on our arm, while eating the treat.

The first bird Allen carried perched on his arm was Della, a common scavenger buzzard. He raised his arm; Della flew off to a nearby tree branch. He then grabbed a piece of meat, held it between his fingers, and raised his arm again. Having a keen vision, Della flew down from the branch, landed on Allen's arm, and ate the food. She then flew to a nearby tree, ready for the next person to offer her a snack. Our next bird was Salim who was a seven-year-old eagle. Allen explained that this type of bird is found in Russia and migrates to Africa. Salim was heavier than the buzzard. I was glad he was a pet.

Following the eagle, Allen produced, Bennie, his 12-year old owl. He explained that owls had five flight feathers on each wing, whereas, hawks have six feathers on each wing. After Allen released Bennie, he advised us to lie on the ground. When the bird saw the meat, he swooped down, barely skimming over our bodies to retrieve his snack.

Finally as we walked further into the field that was surrounded by trees, Allen discussed the Harris hawk. This species was discovered in the Arizona desert by John Audubon who named the fowl, in honor of a friend. This hawk has very long legs, short wings, and is incredibly fast. Henry followed us around like a pet. Allen would signal him to perch in a nearby tree and then he would land on our respective arms. He actually liked to perch, like a parrot, except he was a lot heavier. Allen taught us the way to lift our arms to signal Henry to flight. The activity took about two hours, and we had a splendid time.

We returned to the picnic area where again Allen offered us some refreshment. I thought this was an opportunity to chat, and I relayed my quest to Allen.

Allen said, "There were a lot of mines in this area. Dufton is not far from here. If you like, I am through for the day. I could meet you over there and show you around. Can you meet me at the Red Goose Inn at half past two?"

I discussed this with my parents. Allen jotted down the directions. I drove Mom and Dad back to Langley Castle; they wanted to check out the castle's library. I had just enough time to drive to Dufton and meet Allen at the Red Goose Inn.

Chapter 18~ Dufton Fell~

Allen was waiting at a table on the patio, to the entrance of the Red Goose Inn I when arrived. He stood up and waved to me, "Are you ready to go for a hike?"

"Let me grab a bottle of water." I got a bottle from the trunk of my car and followed Allen a little way through the town of Dufton. Dufton Pike loomed in the background of the village. Ambling through the trailhead which snaked around the outskirts of the village, we traversed multiple gates (signs requesting that gates remained closed). The path crossed several creeks and narrowed at times between the stone fences and trees. A maze of these old, stone fences delineating the mining paths coursed land. Crossing a man-made bridge that was also built with stone, we strolled into an open field. The signposts to Cross Fell led to another opening in a stone fence, and another creek that was lined with trees. Allen pointed out the remains of an old smelt mill. Higher up on the mountainside, I viewed entrances to several mines that were no longer in operation. At the summit of the Great Dunfell stood an old mining entrance, long closed due to cave-ins. Allen said that the miners lived in Dufton because this was a popular area for mining because of the proximity, until the lead veins were mined out. Then miners had to travel farther and stayed away from home during the week and came home on the weekends, leaving their wives and children to maintain the farms.

Allen walked up to the entrance of the mine and peered inside with his flashlight. The opening was a stone archway. "From the looks of this entrance, it is old enough to be one of the ones that your ancestors would have mined." He added, "When the mine entrances did not seem safe, the entrance was constructed with stone and mortar instead of wood timbers. "

"Wow!" I wish we could get a closer look inside". Allen examined the boards at the entrance and after further investigation with his flashlight, he ducked beneath the first board and motioned me to follow him. There was a shaft of light in the near distance which illuminated part of the mine shaft wall.

"It won't be safe to go any farther, but if you look down there on the right, there is a small vein of feldspar crystals." Allen shone his flashlight in that direction, and I could see the shiny reflections. "The miners chiseled them out for their spar boxes. We had better leave now. I wouldn't want to get stuck in here."

As we left the mining entrance, I said," Thank you so much for showing me this. I never would have been able to find this on my own".

Allen replied, "You are most welcome. Let's head back to the Red Goose Inn for a drink." We walked back to the Inn and went inside. The Inn was built in the 1800s. There were several tables outside and there was a sign that said there was a garden out back. It was a quaint building with several sets of tables and chairs. To the right was a fireplace, and in the back was a bar and kitchen. To the left of the entrance was an office and stairs that led up to several rooms for rent. There were a lot of hikers this time of year and this was a good place to eat and rest.

The Inn had many framed maps on the wall. One was a map of Dufton in the year 1600. There was a caption that mentioned that the town's origin was thought to be as early as 670. It also mentioned that there was a Roman milestone along the road near Dufton, suggesting that the Romans had mined lead and silver here during the reign of Emperor Hadrian in 71 AD The town was called Dufton as early as 1175, after Robert de Dufton. There was also a map of Dufton Fell which documented the location of the old mines. In the two neighboring counties of Westmoreland (Westmoreland and Cumberland combined in 1971 and formed County Cumbria) and Durham, there were numerous mining sites. I read somewhere that there had been around 120 mines in these areas.

Allen exchanged greetings with the folks that were there. We ordered some apple pie with ice cream and some more water. While we ate, I asked Allen a ton of questions.

"What is a fell?" I queried.

"A fell is a hill, "Allen explained. "The Pennines are formed by numerous hills or "fells". The villages of Knock and Milburn which are near Dufton, is west of Dunfell, one of the larger hills in the Pennine mountain range. Stake Beck is a stream that runs from Dunnfell into the River Tees, which flows to the coast. The West Pennines had veins or lead ore, iron ore and barites. After the lead is mined, it has to be smelted."

"Who owned the mines? "

Allen continued. "Wealthy landowners, like Lord Thanet, who lived in this area.

"Is that who my Thomas would have worked for?"

"That is a possibility. Around 1820, the local miners partnered together and "take notes" meaning they would lease the land for about a year. The London Lead Company took over the leases here in about 1820. Here in Dufton, they constructed a school, a library and a water system for the families of the miners. The Company had already acquired leases just a bit from here in Alston Moor and Watson."

Allen continued, "One of the differences between the mines here and in Alston was different types of minerals found with the lead ore. Alston veins had fluorspar and the mines here had barite. "

I was full of questions. "What is a hush?"

"The term hushing is when a trench is made and a dam is made at the head. Water was gathered and stored there, then the dam was opened up and the water poured into the trench. The running water wore down the trench to the rock where veins of ore would be found. The miners would be stationed along the trench and pick out the minerals.

"What were the uses for lead?"

"Back then, the major products were roofing, lead shot, paint, piping and other construction materials."

"This is my last mining question for the day, how was the mined lead made into the finished products?"

Allen replied, "The lead was either mined or hushed ...."

"I know what hushed means now!" I added.

"Yes you do!" Allen continued," and then the lead ore was transported by rails in horse-drawn carts to another area where the lead ore was separated from dirt and other rocks, washed, crushed and then sent to a smelting furnace, where the lead would be molded into an ingot. Many of these mines produced silver, which was also smelted along with the lead ore. When the veins of lead had all been mined, the industry virtually ended. Many of the miners had sought employment in the United States – like your ancestors, and also in Spain and Germany.

I explained to Allen about the missing spar box, excluding the part about the money. "I saw the spar box collection at Killhope mining museum. None of them fit the description of the one that I am looking for. Tyler mentioned that there were several museums in County Durham that house some spar boxes. "

"Tyler was referring to Bowes and Weardale."

"Do you think I should plan a trip to those museums?"

Allen said, "Bowes Museum is part of Bernard Castle and there is only one on display there and it is a family piece. The Weardale Museum has a collection of spar boxes from mines in that area; I don't think there would be any from Dufton."

"Do you know of any other place around here that might have a spar box?"

Allen answered, "Local churches might house a spar box that was donated by a family of a miner at the bequest of a deceased miner." That really spurred my attention. My mother had done extensive research on the Newell and Lewis families. She provided me a print-out of the Lewis and Newell names, along with background information and vital statistics that were produced from registries from two local churches.

It was getting on in the day and my feet were quite tired from all the hiking we had done today. I thanked Allen profusely. I was eager to return to the castle and report my findings to my parents.

Chapter 19 ~The Churches~

I awoke bright and early the following morning and borrowed the rental car again. My parents wanted to explore the castle's library and its literary collection. Tyler recommended that I visit a gentleman in Dufton by the name of John Weatherby. He was the church rector at St. Cuthbert's Church. He had preserved vital records back to the 1500s. Tyler jotted down the man's residence in Dufton. He said that everyone in Dufton was a friend of John's, and to inquire at the Red Goose Inn, if I had difficulty locating his flat.

Fairly confident that I had found the proper home. I crossed the large, grassy area in the center of the village, and walked along the sidewalk to one of a series of homes that lined the walkway. I rapped on the door, and after a few seconds, an older, short, heavy-set lady peeked through the opening of the door. She had white hair, pulled back in a bun. Since she didn't recognize me, she just smiled warily and waited for me to say something.

"Hello, my name is Aspen Newby; I am from America and have come to Dufton to research my family history. who were lead miners from this area...."

Before I could finish my sentence, the lady's eyes brightened and she turned her head back toward the house, "John, you have company!" Then she turned to me and said,

"Good day, my name is Jewell, I am John's wife, please come in." She opened the door and escorted me down the hall and to a small den on the left. She called out again, "John, we are in the parlor." She turned to me, "Please, make yourself comfortable; I'll return with some tea." Jewell motioned me to sit down and left the room. I sat down on a well-worn, plaid couch. I looked around the room. There was a fireplace along the main wall and bookshelves lined the remainder of that wall. Along the other wall was an old, roll-top desk with an old miner's lantern.

It wasn't long before Jewell came back with a tray of tea and some biscuits. John followed behind her with several old ledgers in hand. He was a tall, slender gentleman, with gentle eyes, and graying hair. "Hello, there. When Jewell told me you were here, I assumed you came to see these." He was referring to the books that he placed on the coffee table before me. "Where are you from in the states?"

"I am from Georgia, but my mother's family came over from England to Virginia."

John replied, "I have had several visitors who were researching their mining families that were from Virginia, the southwest part, as I recall."

I answered, "Yes. That is where my Lewis and Newell families lived."

"I will be right back, then, I have some papers you might have an interest in. "John then trotted out of the room.

Jewell handed me one of the ledgers. "These are the church records from St. Cuthbert's Church. Maybe you can track down your relatives. Most of the mining families either attended St. Cuthbert's, St. Margaret and St. James Church."

Eagerly, I perused the lists of baptismal, marriages and deaths. The record book began with the 16th century. I had failed to bring anything to take notes on. Jewell realized this and reached in a drawer and handed me some lined paper and a pen. I thanked her and began flipping through the pages, writing down any mention of statistics with the last name of Lewis, Newell or Sutton. There was a host of Lewis's. I leafed through until I found records from the 1700s. I noted the baptismal of Thomas and his siblings, as well as Timothy and Edward Sutton. Beginning in the 1750s, there was a section that listed the church family membership on a yearly basis, similar to a census. I noted that in 1760 Thomas and his family were listed, but not in 1770. The same was true for the Sutton family.

About this time John returned into the room. "I found what I was looking for." He handed me several copies of newsletters from the Little family. Apparently, this family had been here on a genealogy trek several years ago and published a family newsletter of their findings. There were photographs of a mining entrance in Dufton Fell, a little tombstone, and various "people shots". The newsletter contained several articles about their ancestral finds. It was interesting to note that these were descendents of miners as well. Fortunately, there was an email address for the author of the newsletter. I would have to contact them when I found the time.

John told me that he had been a miner in his younger years, and when the veins were exhausted of their lead, he took a job as the local postmaster. He had been the keeper of the church rectory records for years.

I asked John if there were any other churches in the area besides the Catholic churches. He said that there were two Wesleyan churches. There was an old, dilapidated, barn-like building just outside the village that served as the original church. He thought it had been established around 1770 or so. Years later, a larger, brick church was constructed in the village of Dufton and this was the current Wesleyan Methodist church.

Thanking John and Jewell for their hospitality, I arose to leave. John said, "I am not doing anything special today, would you like for me to show you around the churches?"

"Why, yes! That would be wonderful!"

"Let me get my hat and I'll meet you at the car." I wanted to do something for them and remembered some fudge that I had bought at the local market. It was still in the "boot" of the car. I told Jewell that I would be right back, retrieved the fudge and walked back to their home.

"Thank you, Jewell," as I handed her the fudge.

Her eyes widened, and she gave me a gracious smile as she hugged me, "Fudge, my favorite! Thank you!" By this time, James was closing behind her in the hallway, ready to venture out. "Have a good day, luv!" She exclaimed as we strolled to the car.

The first church we visited was just outside Dufton, the St. Margaret and St. James' Church of Long Marton Parish. This parish consisted of three villages, Marton, Brampton and Knock. As is true for just about every religious edifice in England, this church's roots date back to medieval times. According to the records, the church was restored in the late 1800s and was built from red sandstone. As we approached the ancient, wrought iron gates, we could see all the old gravestones from centuries past. The grass was neatly trimmed. The older grave markers were marble aged by rain and wind which had faded the chiseled lettering. Moss had covered the unkempt ones. After coursing our way through the tombstones, we finally found a set of Lewis graves. The stones were virtually illegible, but I could barely make out the Lewis name. I wanted to assume they were Richard and Anne's parents. (Mother actually knew where the cemetery was that the Lewis and Newell families were buried in Virginia.) The church was open to the public. The sanctuary had one center aisle to the pulpit area. On either side were wooden pews. In my opinion, the cemetery surrounding the church was much more interesting to me.

As we left the church, John navigated a short distance down the road between Dufton and Knock, turning down a road at a sign that said St. Cuthbert's Church; it had an arrow pointing the way. The church's structure and grounds were very much like the church in Long Marton. It was a little smaller building, but the same architecture with the cemetery surrounded the church. The interior of the church seemed a little more modern, with a blue runner carpet flowing down the center aisle. The pews were a darker wood and there was a lovely, arched, stained glass window at the altar. The pulpit was to the left of the altar and there were smaller arched, stained glassed windows on each side of the room. Next to the pulpit was an area designated for the choir and across from the pulpit was an old organ. Modern drop lamps hung from the ceiling. There was a small balcony in the rear of the church. I sat down in a pew near the back of the church, wondering if there were designated pews for Thomas' family. Where did the Suttons sit, in the balcony? I once heard that employees of landowners weren't allowed to sit on the main area of a church. I had a sudden feeling of belonging. This is where my family worshipped. As we exited the lovely sanctuary, I grabbed a pamphlet and tossed a couple of English pounds into the donation box that sat at a table near the door. The current church was built in the late 1700s; the original church was erected in the late 13th century. Gee, things were so old in England!   The pamphlet also indicated that many miners from Dufton Fell were buried here.

John was outside searching through the graves while I was inside the church. As I walked out of the foyer, he motioned for me to come over. "Look what I found." He pointed to a simple, marble cross. At the base of the marker I could make out the name of Sutton.   "Isn't that one of the names you were looking for?"

"Yes, yes it is!" There was no date, or first name. Could this be Edward Sutton's final resting place? There were a few other graves around this one, but the markers were long disintegrated or completely missing, the burial sites visible only by the sunken indentation of the ground.   We continued walking through the cemetery. There were a few family plots lined up along the fence of the cemetery facing the main road. They were separated either by brick or stone walls, many of them tumbled down with age. Several had iron fences demarcating the plots of land. Engraved at the entrance of one of these plots was the name of Graves. Not wanting to disturb the site, I peered through the gate and saw the markers of Sally and her brothers, along with her parents. Sally had never married! I wondered if word had ever gotten to Thomas that Sally remained a spinster. How sad. I had walked around the entire cemetery and found many burial plots of the Lewis family. Mr. Weatherby's records from St. Cuthbert's were full of Lewis's.

On our drive back, John suggested we drive out in the countryside as he pointed out several places of interest. While we were driving, I told James the story of the spar box. Being a miner in his earlier years, he was familiar with spar boxes. I asked him if any of the churches around here had any spar boxes, since, obviously there were none visible in the churches we had visited. "I am not aware of any, but then again, I am Catholic and haven't been on the insides of these Wesleyan churches. We will stop by the post office and I will ask the postmaster. "James toured me around the various shops and homes in Dufton, and showed me places I would never have found on my own. When we arrived at the post office, I plopped down on a park bench and sipped some water. When he returned, John indicated that the Wesleyan church was open during the week and there was a church secretary there that could help us.

We drove to the Methodist chapel in town. It was a brick building, with an arched front door and two arched windows on either side. Over the arched door was a circular window that looked like a glass daisy. There was a middle-aged lady standing on the walkway to greet us. "Hello, my name is Lucy Brenner, I am the church secretary. I live next door. The postmaster called me and asked me to meet you here. We introduced ourselves and followed her as she opened the door to the foyer, leading us inside. The chapel was small inside, in comparison to the others we had visited today. The floors were covered with red carpe, with white walls. The wooden pews were a lighter color, and the hanging lamps looked the same as those at St. Cuthbert's. The pulpit was in the center of the front wall. There was a fresh flower arrangement on the altar, in front of the pulpit. There was a piano to the left of the pulpit. The ceiling had wooden trim, the same color as the pews.

We sat in one of the pews and conversed for a few minutes. "My ancestors were lead miners from this area. I have found evidence of their membership at St. Cuthbert's in 1760, but not 1770. I know they were Methodists when they came to Virginia in the early 1800s. Do you have any old records here?
"

Lucy replied, "We have a room behind the sanctuary that serves as a small library. I believe the original record books are back there. Come with me," she said as she arose and walked to the back of the church, opened the rear door and entered a room with a table, chairs and several bookcases. She rummaged around several old books and pulled out a dusty ledger. "Here it is," she said as she opened it and leafed through the initial pages. "The first record of membership is listed in 1770, but not in this church; that would have the initial membership of the first Wesleyan church that this one replaced." She handed me the book.

My heart skipped a beat when I read the names of Thomas, John, Ann, and their parents, John and Elizabeth Lewis. The list was alphabetical, I perused down to the S's. There he was! Timothy Sutton! "Lucy, I queried, "Where was the first church? Is it still standing?"

"The first church is now a dilapidated old barn building out in the countryside."

"Can we visit it?"

"It is private property now. You would have to get in touch with the landowner to visit inside, but I suppose you could have a look inside through a window." Upon leaving Dufton, our route took us to the original church that looked like an old barn. I remember that we had passed by this building earlier in the day. There was no signage there, so it could easily go unnoticed to passersby. We stopped and took a peek in one of the windows of the old church building and the main room was empty. I couldn't help but think that maybe there was a basement or closet or attic that might be the home of the missing spar box. Later I would ask Tyler if he could find out who owned the property and get permission for us enter the building.

Chapter 20 ~Allen Dent's Predicament~

Within the confines of my wood paneled study, I pondered my encounter with Aspen Blair. Why did she have such an interest in this spar box? They were exquisite in their own right; a tribute to a passing era. Local craftsmen started producing spar boxes, and she could have purchased one of these. But why would someone venture so far to pursue an old spar box? Most of them had no great monetary value.

I had an interest in genealogy, archiving my family history gathered over the years by various relatives. Like most locals in the surrounding counties, I descended from mining families. "I haven't looked at these files in years," I reminded myself, as I scooted my chair away from the walnut desk, and opened the old, dusty, file cabinet that I had retrieved from my attic. I started perusing through the folders of old family papers arranged by surname. I stared at my own name, Dent. My grandfather, Dennis and my father, Wilbur, were lead miners. After the lead industry came to a halt, my father and many of his coworkers took up coal mining. I continued to go back in the family tree through several generations of miners. Dennis's parents were Jackson and Katie Dent. Katie was the daughter of Timothy and Rachel Sutton.

I lifted the yellowish-tan, leather-bound family Bible and gently placed it on the desk. The Holy Bible was engraved in gold, and in the center of the cover had Mary Louise Sutton etched in smaller letters. The spine was loosely attached from years of wear. At the beginning of the Old Testament were several thicker and more ornate pages notating Births, Marriages and Deaths. Between the Old and New Testaments was the Apocryphal Books, five of the recognized sixteen texts. These books are non-canonical; all but one thought to be written during Old Testament days. These books were permanently omitted by 1827. At the beginning of that section, there was a page dedicated to Notable Events. The handwriting of the names varied in script from generations posting their lineage.

Mary Louise Sutton passed the family Bible down to her son, Timothy Sutton, when he married Rachel Lindsey. Rachel had continued the documentation of the vital statistics, but Timothy had placed an entry under Notable Events. He put a mark after the date of his brother's death that his mother had entered. Next to the mark, he scribed in small letters, "see NE". I was intrigued by this because I could not locate the Notable Events page in the Bible. Not until I decided to look in the Table of Contents, I discovered that NE was the abbreviation for the Notable Events page and its location in the Apocrypha, meaning hidden things. Was it a coincidence that Timothy had selected this page to make his notation? Here, Timothy briefly surmised, in minute print, at the foot of the page, "E set up T and stole money. I found, and hid it.. Sent T letter and key."

My mind raced. "I must find out more about why Aspen is here. She must know about the money. Timothy must have hidden it in a spar box," I surmised. "I'll see if I can get Tyler to pry it out of her." I continued to think, "If that money is gold or silver coins, it would be worth a fortune now I have got to find that spar box first! I have just as much right to that money as she does! Should I tell Tyler what I know, or let him lead me to it?"

Chapter 21 ~Hadrian's Wall~

The following morning, I ate with my parents, thoroughly enjoying the sumptuous English breakfast. My dish was filled with bacon, grilled mushrooms and tomatoes, oatmeal, toast and a poached egg. Thankfully, in addition to tea, coffee was also served. I definitely could adjust to the formality of the Brits, each meal served on china and with sterling silver flatware on top of a white, starched table cloth and linen napkins, with fresh flowers as the centerpiece. It was quite a contrast to most continental breakfasts served in hotels back in the states, with the Styrofoam plates and cups, plastic utensils and paper napkins. Coffee never tastes good in Styrofoam.

My parents and I shared stories of the events of our past few days. They were going to visit a World War II air museum that was not far away in Yorkshire. Tyler was going to pick me up after breakfast to visit a section of Hadrian's Wall in Northumberland.

Tyler arrived up shortly after breakfast. We traveled to a lovely little village called Bardon Mill. We pulled into the car park (a parking lot in America) in front of the General Store/Post Office in the quaint town. In front of the building on either side of the entrance were large planters loaded with colorful flowers. We purchased some snacks for our day of hiking. At the check-out counter, I asked the cashier (and postal worker), "Do you have any Altoids? "

He answered, "Altoids? What are they?"

I replied, "You know, the ones that are in a tin box, the "curiously strong mint. It says they are from England on the tin."

The cashier mused," Ah, yes, I do recall a chap who had a box of the mints and offered me a peppermint, and it was very strong. He explained that peppermint was the only flavor available in England now, and he could only find them in London. He added that they were now manufactured in the States, Tennessee, I recollect and that there were many flavors available there.'

During this time, Tyler was searching the web on his cell phone and chimed in, "They originated in England in1780, and soon were manufactured in Wales. Wrigley is now the manufacturer and, yes, they are manufactured in Chattanooga, Tennessee. It also says they are hard to find in England as they are now imported. "

The friendly sales clerk offered, "I have some fine English mints here," as he reached inside the counter and pulled out a tray of individually-wrapped mints, "Might I recommend these Everton Mints by Barker and Dobson?" He selected one of the black and white mints, "Try one," he offered.

"Thank you, I replied, unwrapping the mint, and popped it into my mouth. I exclaimed, "Wow that is a great flavor! I'll buy some of these!" Tyler and I made our purchases and walked out to the car and headed northeast from Barton Mill on B6138.

Tyler said," I thought that I would take you to see a section of Hadrian's Wall. It is not far from here".

"Wasn't it a Roman outpost?"

Taylor replied, "It is a little more than that. It spans across Northern England about 70 miles. We are going to Housestead's Fort." We didn't have to go far and we turned into the park. Upon entering the park office and small museum, there was a display with various pamphlets. After browsing a few of them while Tyler talked with the attendant, I learned a few tidbits. Housestead's Fort is property of the National Trust and maintained by the English Heritage. This English charity organization protects historical places by public funding. The English Heritage is a government-funded organization that maintains the historic sites. Construction began in AD 122. It took six years to build and was built to monitor the coming and going of folks and to keep the "barbarians" out. Originally, the wall was 15 ft high and 10 feet thick, but is much smaller than that today due to erosion. There were 30 forts with Milecastles placed at every Roman mile. Housestead's Roman Fort (its Roman name was Vercovicium) covers five acres, is one of the most intact, and has many remaining buildings. Foundations remain from a hospital, barracks, bath house and latrines. In contrast to other forts along the Wall, Housestead's did not have

129

running water. It is thought that the soldiers gathered rainwater from large receptacles. The attendant visited the Roman ruins in Ephesus, Turkey and shared an interesting story about the latrines. The latrines were like benches with multiple "toilets" side-by-side, and the seats were carved into a slab of marble. There was a trench underneath where the refuse exited. He noted that it was so cold in Northern England in the winter that if the Romans used marble seats, they would literally stick to the seats! So they carved seats from wood.

We made our way through the turnstile and entered the park. This was my first visit to a ruin and I was fascinated. What I saw was mostly square or rectangular areas with lots of rocks piled here and there.   There were little historical markers at the base of each edifice, describing what the building use to be and an artist's rendering of what the building might have looked like 2000 years ago. I could only determine the latrine structure.

After walking to each building while taking a few pictures, Tyler pointed to the outskirts of the fort. "Let's go check out the Wall", he said as we trekked around the grounds. We walked to the stone wall which was about six feet high. There was an area where we could step up to the top and walk down the Wall before the stones sloped down toward the ground again. The view was stunning; it overlooked an escarpment with a deep valley and green pastureland which turned into massive woods.

I imagined the Scots hiding in this forest waiting to gain access into the fort. With this view, the Roman garrisons would have no trouble defending their stronghold.

I decided that it was as good a time as any to raise the subject with Tyler about the abandoned church in Dufton. "Tyler," I started, "yesterday, I met up with John Weatherby in Dufton. Do you know him?"

Tyler thought for a minute, "Isn't he the man who is the curator of St. Cuthbert's Church?"

"Yes," I answered, "He was kind enough to show me around Dufton and several of the churches yesterday." I continued to tell him about our visit with the church secretary at the Methodist church and her routing us to the older, abandoned church. "Lucy said that we would need permission to enter the older church since it was on private property. Do you happen to know who owns that land?"

"I know the building you are talking about. I don't know who owns it but I am sure my uncle will know. I'll give him a ring when I return home."

We finished touring the grounds and made our way back to the car. I couldn't wait to hear back from Tyler after he talked to his uncle.

Chapter 22~Allen Dent's Deception~

I was sorting through some boxes that I had carried from the attic when there was a knock at the door. I opened the door to find Tyler. After the usual exchange of greetings, Tyler said, "You seem preoccupied, Uncle. Is there something I can help you with?"

"I have been feeling a bit nostalgic," he lied," I have been sorting through some old family papers and photographs. What have you been up to today?"

"I wanted to see Aspen again, so I invited her to see Hadrian's Wall."

Allen asked, "Did you two have a good time?"

"Ah, yes, I rather fancy her. I want to see her as much as I can before she returns to the States."

I continued, "When is she leaving?"

"I don't know. She hasn't discussed it and I don't want to ask her. Uncle, do you know that old Methodist church that looks like a barn near Dufton, do you know who owns the property?"

My interest was piqued. "Why, yes, I do. Why do you inquire?"

Tyler added, "Aspen is interested in visiting inside the church."

"Is there any particular reason?" I tried to act nonchalant.

"She didn't say really. She said that Mr. Weatherby from Dufton has been showing her around the old churches and cemeteries, and she wanted to know if she could see inside the old church."

"I do recall Aspen asking me about the spar boxes and where they might be located locally. I told her sometimes churches or libraries housed them. I'll give Henry a ring and see if I can schedule a time for us to meet him there."

Tyler replied, "That would be great! Let me know the arrangements and I'll pass them on to Aspen." We made small talk for the next few minutes. I feigned a headache from reading all the old documents. Tyler thanked me for my assistance and bade me good goodbye.

As soon as Tyler left, I called my friend, Henry Clayton. "Henry, how are you?"

"As well as could be expected," Henry replied, "it's been a long time since I spoke to you." We chitchatted for a few minutes.

"The reason for my call, Henry, is to ask you if you still own the property where the old Methodist church stands."

"I do, and I am trying to sell it, are you interested?" Henry queried.

I wasn't aware that the property was for sale. Up until last night, I would not have been interested. "I have been considering it," he let on, "Could we set up a time to look at the property... and could you show me inside the old church as well?"

"How about tomorrow before it gets too hot, say 9 AM."

"That would be splendid," I answered, making sure not to sound too excited.

I promptly arrived at the location of the old church the following, morning a few minutes before Henry. We exchanged pleasantries as we walked a short distance to what looked like an old barn. The grounds had remained unkempt and there was a great deal of overgrowth of bushes and trees surrounding the building as well as ivy that had practically taken over the entranceway. Henry unlatched the door and we entered the old church. The main room was almost barren, except for the remnants of a pulpit which was in the far left corner. If there had been pews, they had been removed years before. The hardwood flooring crackled underneath our footfalls. There were two sets of windows on either wall of the room. There was a doorway on the other end of the main room that opened into a smaller area. Inside the smaller room was a door that opened into a closet. In the opposite corner to the closet was a set of stairs that descended to a basement of sorts. Henry said there were stacks of old planks and bricks down there. We didn't have a flashlight, so our tour ended here. We traced our way back to the sanctuary and Henry showed me around the surrounding grounds.

After I returned home, I thought about purchasing the old church property. The only part we didn't explore was the basement. Owning the building had its benefits, if Aspen found anything of any value in the basement, or she tried to take anything out, without my permission, that would be stealing. On the other hand, if she didn't find anything, then it would cost me my investment, because the property was not very marketable. I remembered that Tyler expected me to call him back regarding arrangements for Aspen to inspect the old church. I decided to give it some thought and make my decision in the morning.

I awoke the following morning after a restless sleep. At this point, I didn't want Tyler to know the nature of my encounter with Henry. I decided to call Henry and explain that my nephew had a friend from the States that fancies old architecture. I asked if Tyler could set up an appointment with him to see the property. I emphasized to Henry that Tyler was unaware that I had an interest in purchasing the land, and would he keep that information private. Henry agreed with my plan and we scheduled a time for Tyler and Aspen to meet him at the church.

I called Tyler and relayed then appointment time for this afternoon.

Chapter 23~ The Old Church~

Tyler called me and explained that his uncle had arranged an appointment with the owner of the property, Henry Clayton, to see inside the old church. Tyler and I met with Mr. Clayton on Sunday afternoon at the building. I remembered to bring a couple of flashlights since the building would probably not have too much light shining through the windows to illuminate the interior.

We introduced ourselves, and Mr. Clayton led the way through undergrowth and trees to the entrance. There must have been a cleared path years ago, but you wouldn't know it now. Since it was early in the day, there was enough light to see the entirety of the sanctuary. I spied an old pulpit and ventured to inspect it. Of course, there was nothing there but inches of dust and dead bugs. Mr. Clayton showed us another smaller room where there was a set of stairs.

"I would like to go downstairs," I said.

Mr. Clayton replied, "I'm not too sure how safe those old steps are," and he added, "there is nothing down there except some old bricks and wood."

"I would like to see down there anyway." I cut my flashlight on and examined the first step. The second step was missing. Indeed, the descent would be a challenge.

Tyler said, "Isn't there an entrance on the lower side of the barn?"

"Yes, there is, if we can get down there through the overgrowth," answered Mr. Clayton.

"I am game, let's try," I responded.

Mr. Clayton said, "I'm too old for that, I'll gladly wait for you in my car. I could use a nap!"

Mr. Clayton handed Tyler the keys as we left the church and headed around the back of the building, while Mr. Clayton made his way back to his car. We stayed close to the building and were able to dodge any major scratches from unruly branches and vines. We tried to open the door without a key, but it would not budge. Tyler tried the two keys that were on the ring, and neither one would open the old keyhole lock on the door. I saw on TV that someone used a Bobbie pin to pick a lock. I didn't have a Bobbie pin, but did have a hair clip, maybe it would work. I poked the pointed end of the clip into the hole and turned the knob. The keyhole seemed to have some play in it; so I started jiggling the clip in the lock, pushing in and out on the door while turning the knob. After repeating this routine several times, the door actually opened!

It was a good thing we had our flashlights. There were several glass-less windows on either side of the room which was dimly lit. Near the rotten stairs on the far side of the room was a pile of old timbers and bricks. "Since we have gotten this far, we might as well take a look around," I said to Tyler. We circled around the stack of wood, pulled on several of the boards and found nothing. I walked over to the bricks stacked against the far wall. As I approached it, I realized it was an old fire place, dusty with ashes. I grabbed a smaller piece of wood from the pile and started poking around the ashes. There were few partially burned papers; apparently the fire had died down before all the trash had burned. I felt something more substantial than papers. "Hey, Tyler, bring your flashlight over here, I think I have found something!"

Tyler walked over, shining his light down into the fireplace. I used the stick to push what I found away from the ashes. What I found was a partially burned and charred old ledger. "I hope the insides aren't too destroyed. Let's go outside where there is light. We crossed back through the room, exiting the basement. I didn't have anything to clean the book; I grabbed some leaves from a nearby branch. My hands were pretty dirty. Luckily, the two things that I always carried in my jeans pockets were lip balm and a small bottle of hand sanitizer. After cleaning my hands, and Tyler's, too, I examined the book more carefully.

The pages of the ledger were fairly well intact. They were charred along the edges; most of the pages were readable. Its contents seemed to be a list of items purchased for the church, where purchased and the cost. As I flipped through the pages, there was also a section that looked like an inventory of items, including furniture and such. I didn't have time to peruse the whole book, so I asked Tyler, "I would like to take this home and look over it. Do you think Mr. Clayton would mind? I can give it to you to return to him."

"I don't think he will object; he seems like a rather nice chap", Tyler responded.

We locked the door back and traipsed our way back to the entrance of the building. Mr. Clayton seemed to be asleep in his car. As Tyler rapped on the front door, he awoke, rolled down his window and said, "Hello, as he yawned, I was just catnapping. Any luck getting in the lower door? "

"Yes, we were able to open the door (I didn't go into detail), and I found this ledger in the fireplace. I was wondering if I could borrow it for the evening and then give it to Tyler to return to you."

'That will be fine," Mr. Clayton responded, "Tyler can give it to his uncle to return to me."

"Thank you very much! I am sure I will enjoy reading through it."

Tyler and I thanked Mr. Clayton for showing us the old church and we walked back to Tyler's car. After we got into the vehicle, I asked, "Is there a library nearby? If I find anything interesting in this book, I would like to make some photocopies of the pages."

"There is a library in Appleby, which is not far from here. It is a quaint little town. We could go there, stop at a coffee shop, and look over the ledger there. We could walk to the library from there if you want to make any copies."

"Splendid! I would love some coffee, and maybe they will have blueberry scones!"

Chapter 24~ Appleby Coffee Shop~

We took a leisurely drive through the countryside toward Appleby. Pastures protected with ancient stone fences flanked on both sides of the narrow road; it did not seem to be wide enough for two-way traffic. The B6542 took us to Appleby. Driving to Bridge Street, we crossed the Eden River. We steered onto Boroughgate, the only street in Appleby, coursing north to south, and one of the widest streets in England.

Riding through town, Tyler gave me a short history lesson. The North end consists of the St. Lawrence Church and the Low Cross, and at the South End stands Appleby Castle and the High Cross. These structures are monuments, not crosses. They were erected at each end of the street to mark scaffolding placed to hold festivities during the time that Lady Anne Clifford lived in Appleby Castle in the late 1600s. She was influential in restoring buildings in the town after England's Civil War. She was a descendant of the Clifford Family who owned the Appleby Castle dating back to 1300. The Tourist Information Center is in a building that dates back to1596. The houses and shops lining both sides of the street date back to the 17th century. Old lime trees shade the area around the Eden River, including the dwellings and shops.

Tyler spied a parking spot on the street. "There is a coffee shop right over there," he said, as he pointed to a row of buildings along the street. The white stone building was trimmed in brown woodwork. Before leaving the car, Tyler found a towel in the trunk, using it to protect the ledger. Climbing several steps we opened the door, entering the establishment. The room was bright and sunny, with several sets of tables and chairs arranged between bookshelves on either side. We selected a spot near the window. After placing our order, I excused myself to the bathroom where I dusted off the book as best I could with a damp paper towel. Satisfied that it would not shed excessive dust, I returned to the table. I opened the ledger and began to look through it.

The first entry dated 15 March 1770 was titled "Initial Inventory". Listed were 8 pews, 1 pulpit, one altar table, and 15 song books borrowed from (I could not make out the rest of the sentence here). On 7 June 1770, the second page documented the following: brick fire place completed, steps completed, new door placed. The following pages itemized yearly inventory, purchases, and repairs. A separate section notated weekly tithes and monthly tallies. Toward the end of the ledger there was a section of items donated – wall hangings, plaques, flowers, and the last item, caught my eye - a spar box, donated by R. Sutton in memory of T. Sutton! I glanced back at the top of the page to find the date - 20 December 1820. If my memory served me correctly, the year of Timothy's letter to Thomas was 1810. Ten years had lapsed. Was this the same spar box? Who was R. Sutton? What was the relation to T. Sutton? I wondered who had moved the spar box and where was it now?

I shared these findings with Tyler. "Am I getting closer to finding the spar box, or just wasting time? I am so frustrated!" Rambling on, I didn't notice an elderly gentleman approach our table. I stopped chattering and said, "I'm sorry, I am probably too loud."

"No, not at all," he said, "My name is Hugh Lindsey, the owner of this shop", as he extended his hand.

As we shook hands, I replied, "Nice to meet you, my name is Aspen Blair and this is my friend, Tyler Dent." Mr. Lindsey looked like he might be my grandfather's age. He was tall, but a little stooped. He still had a head full of well-trimmed, dark hair and had kind eyes. He was dressed in khakis and a white Oxford shirt.

"I couldn't help but overhear your conversation, and when I heard the you speak of a spar box donated by R. Sutton, …well, my great-great-grandfather was Albert Lindsey, and his sister was Rachel Lindsey Sutton. "

"Could this be the person who is listed in this ledger? Do you know who she married?

"From where did you get the ledger?" he asked.

"I found it at this old church, but it looked more like a barn, in Dufton."

"I see, "he said, "Do you mind if I pull up a chair?"

"No, of course, not, please join us". We scooted over to make room for a third chair at the table.

Mr. Lindsey asked, "What brings you to Northern England, Aspen? "

"Well, the short story is that I am looking for a spar box that was mentioned in a letter to my great, great ,great ... I am not sure how far back, great –uncle, Thomas Newell, written by Timothy Sutton, back in 1810. Timothy made it as a gift for him. Thomas never made it back to England to accept it. I located the names of the Newell and Sutton families in a church registry, from the late 1700s, which led me to the old church."

Mr. Lindsey listened intently, and said, "Rachel was married to Timothy Sutton. This bookstore used to be owned by Rachel's father. It has been in the Lindsey family for all these years. The building was dormant for years, and after I graduated from the University, I began renovating the building and reopened it as a coffee house and a bookstore. I have a collection of books that were published in the late 1700s and early 1800s that shared a space on Rachel and Timothy's bookshelf." Mr. Lindsey arose, and said, "I'll be back in a minute,"

I was so excited, "Tyler, do you think he has the spar box?" Before Tyler could respond, Mr. Lindsey returned to the table with a Bible.

Mr. Lindsay sat down again and explained that it was customary for people to maintain dates of birth, death and marriages in family Bibles. He opened the Bible and showed us where Emily Lindsey documented the dates of birth and marriage of Rachel and Timothy, Jr, as well as the births of her grandchildren. Over the decades, the Bible was passed down to Hugh, and he indicated where he entered the births of his children, as well as the deaths of his parents. "And that is how I know Rachel and Timothy Sutton!"

Tyler had been reading over the records, "What a minute," he said, "I see here where Rachel and Timothy had a child name Katie and she married Jackson Dent. I wonder if we are related. It doesn't' look like anyone kept up with Rachel and Timothy's descendents. "

"That is because it is a Lindsay family tree, and there won't be much documentation about the Sutton branch, "Mr. Lindsey replied, "Dent is a fairly common name in this area, who is your father?"
"My father was Geoffrey Dent, but my parents were killed in a car accident a few years ago.. His brother is Allen Dent, do you know him?"

"Ah, yes, Allen. So he is your uncle! It is a small world!"

I brought conversation back to my current issue, "Mr. Lindsey, do you know anything about what happened to the spar box?"

"Tyler's Uncle Allen has it; he just isn't aware of this fact."

Chapter 25 ~Hugh Lindsay's Story~

Hugh began his story, and we listened intently. "Timothy and Rachel were married in 1812. They had two children Katie and Timothy Jr. Her husband died of consumption in 1819. Rachel moved back with her parents to raise her two small children. She had to sell most of their furniture and she donated Timothy's spar box to the Wesleyan Church in Dufton. Timothy had told Rachel that Thomas Newell, or someone from his family might call on her one day, looking for the spar box that he had made as a gift to Thomas. Rachel told Timothy, Jr about the spar box when he was old enough to understand and that it was at the church, should someone from America come inquiring about it. Years passed and turned into decades and no one from America ever came to retrieve the spar box. "

"In 1850, Rachel died at age.61. Many of the Sutton and Lindsey families attended the funeral. Timothy Sutton, Jr was prosperous and had a fine country home. He invited all of the cousins for lunch before they left for their respective homes. The Wesleyan church had been abandoned and a new one constructed in town. There was no room for the donated spar box, and the preacher asked the Sutton family if they wanted the spar box. Timothy, Jr did not particularly want it, but being a part of mining history in that area, he asked the Sutton and Lindsey cousins if they wanted to make a donation to the church in exchange for the spar box. My ancestor, Archie Lindsey, was the first to express an interest in it, so he obtained the spar box, donating a fine sum to the church. When Archie died, the spar box was left to my grandfather. When my grandfather passed away, he left it to my cousin, Wilbur Dent, now a coal miner, but was familiar with spar boxes because he previously mined lead. When Wilbur inherited the spar box, he erected a wooden box to protect it, and put it in his attic for safe keeping until his boys grew up. Wilbur was ailing. His son, Geoffrey, had died in an automobile accident. Allen was a bachelor so he moved back in with his father to take care of him, and he still lives there. He probably has no idea that the spar box is in his attic. "

Tyler responded, "Isn't it ironic that we have been searching for this spar box and all along, it has been under our noses! Aspen, I think our next stop is Uncle Allen's house."

I couldn't believe that we actually were this close to the spar box. I never dreamed that we would find it. The letter and the key were safely stored with my father, who never loses anything. I had not told Tyler about the hidden money, if it was still there at all. Hugh had not made mention of any hidden money. Any of the family who had possession of the spar box could have confiscated the money, but surely there would have been a story passed down through the family. Was it possible that the hidden drawer in the spar box was still a secret? I decided to wait and see the spar box and then decide what to do next. "Okay, Tyler, I'm ready to go; do we need to see if Allen is home first?"

"No," he replied, "I have a key to his house if he is not home. "

We thanked Mr. Lindsey for the invaluable information, paid for our coffee and scones and headed out to the car.

Chapter 26 ~Tyler's Loyalty Challenged~

"I don't know how my uncle will take this," I said as we drove along.

"Do you think the spar box is still in the attic?" Aspen questioned.

"I don't know. Sometimes he is very possessive of his things. I don't think he is aware of the spar box in his attic, because he has not mentioned it to you or me, and you have made it clear that you are looking for it. When we get to the house, I think it would be best if you remain in your seat if we see that his car is there." It took about 15-20 minutes to drive to Allen's home. Allen's car was in the driveway. As promised, Aspen sat in the car. "I'll come back as soon as I can," I said.

I knocked on the door, finding it unlocked, I entered. "Uncle Allen? Hello?"

"I am in my study, Tyler."

"Don't get up, I'll come to you." I didn't want him to happen by the front window, noticing Aspen in the car. I walked down the hall and turned into the well-used study. It was lined with wooden bookcases, a comfortable couch suitable for afternoon naps, and two, large upholstered chairs. There was a computer desk and chair in the corner. I found Allen sitting at his computer.

Allen turned in his swivel chair, smiled and pointed to the couch, "Have a seat and tell me about your morning."

I didn't want to keep Aspen waiting long, and succinctly telling him about Aspen finding the ledger at the church, and that Mr. Clayton let us borrow it. I continued with our trip to Appleby, the coffee shop, explaining our discovery of the spar box and R. Sutton. Finally, I informed Allen about the good fortune of meeting Hugh Lindsey, a descendant of Rachel Sutton's brother, and our own family connection with the Suttons.

Uncle Allen listened intently. "So I have a long, lost cousin, "he pondered.

"Yes, and here's the best part. Mr. Lindsey said that Rachel was the wife of Timothy Sutton, who made the spar box for Thomas Lewis, Aspen's ancestor. "

"Did he know what happened to the spar box?"

I explained as best as I could remember the story that Hugh had told us. Your father ended up with it, and, apparently it is crated up in your attic in this very house!"

"What? Why didn't he tell me or your father about it? "

"Hugh said that when Wilbur inherited the spar box, it was prior to your returning home to take care of him after his stroke. He probably forgot about it. "

"Well, I know what I am going to do today."

Tyler said, "Aspen is sitting out in my car. May I ask her to come in?"

"Take her back to her lodgings and come back here and help me find the crate," Allen said rather curtly.

"Yes, of course, but may I ask why?"

"Just give her a lift, come back here, and I'll tell you why."

I went back to the car, quite perturbed at my Uncle. Aspen read the troubled look on my face as I got into the car. "Well?" she asked.

"I told my uncle about what happened today. When I got to the part about the spar box probably being in his attic, he seemed to get wild-eyed, like he was surprised and mad at the same time. When I told him you were out here and could I ask you to come in, he told me to take you home and come back to the house. When I asked why he said he would explain when I returned."

"That is just odd, but, okay. I probably need to spend some time with my parents."

Tyler added, "I'll give you a ring when I find out what is going on." We got back to the castle. She leaned over, gave me a hug and said, "Thanks for helping me out. See you later."

Chapter 27 ~Allen Dent's Attic~

After Tyler left the house, I had a decision to make before his return. He is my brother's only child. I must be honest with him; I am sure he will understand. I will wait for his return before venturing to the attic. It will be like a treasure hunt or Christmas Day! I might even give him some of the money we find.

When Tyler returned, we went into the study again; I presented the Sutton Family Bible. "I want to show you something, Tyler, "I said as I opened the book. I turned to the bookmarked Notable Events page. "Look here", I pointed to the passage - E set up T and stole money. I found, and hid it. Sent T letter and key.

"What does this mean?" Tyler asked.

"From what I can tell, E is Edward, Timothy's brother. Apparently he set up someone whose name begins also with T and stole the money. Timothy found the money and hid it from Edward. Then he says he sent T a letter and a key. This T person must be Aspen's ancestor, Thomas Lewis. He received a letter from Timothy with a key that probably opens the spar box that Aspen is looking for. We need to see if   that money is still there."

"Aspen has never mentioned any money, or a key," Tyler responded," she only referred to the letter."

I replied," If I were Aspen, do you think that I would travel all the way to Appleby, from the States, looking for a long, lost spar box, unless I surmised money was hidden in it? Do you think I would tell anyone I knew about hidden money? Of course not! She has to know about this wealth! The difference is that the spar box is apparently hidden in my attic. We are going to find it first. We will find the currency, and remove it from the spar box. I will give you a portion of the money as a finder's fee. Then you can inform Aspen that we found the spar box, sans the money. If she wants the spar box, she can have it for sentimental reasons."

"But Uncle that money belongs to Aspen!"

"Not if I find it first. Are you with me or not? You can either help me, or leave now!"

I raised my voice more than I should have. I could see that my nephew was taken aback by my tone. Tyler had a decision to make. "I'll help you out," Tyler replied.

"That's my boy," I said, as I gave him a pat on the shoulder, "Let's go find that spar box."

We walked down the hall and up the stairs to the second story. The upstairs had a guest bedroom, a bath, and a door that opened into another large area that was the attic. My father had never finished this enormous room, and thought it would be a great storage area. He had been a pack rat and never one to

155

rid of anything, including my mother's storage. He had placed rods on one end to keep seasonal clothing. Both had been dead for years and I had never thought much about cleaning out the room, since I had never married and had no use for the extra space. Lumber was stacked inside, Christmas decorations, camping equipment, and lots of furniture. There was barely room to walk. There was a bookshelf on the right as we entered the room. I located the Bible on the first shelf. There were boxes and crates everywhere. Prior to a couple of days ago, I had not visited the attic in years. It was hot and musty. I told Tyler to start opening crates and boxes on the left side of the room, and I would work on the other side. I had no idea the size of this crate. Tyler and I chatted back and forth as we opened boxes, finding fabric, toys, china, old crocheted blankets, quilts, and military artifacts, to name a few things. I never knew there was so much stuff up here. It would be a veritable gold mine on EBay!

Sweating profusely, our shirts showed signs of perspiration. Wiping cobwebs from a dated chair, I took a breather while Tyler trotted downstairs for bottles of water, I sorted some items that were of value, and told Tyler to move these out into the bedroom across the hall. This afforded us ample walking space in the attic. Digging around for an hour or so, I came upon an old crate. "Tyler", I called, "Come over here, I think I might have found our spar box!" Tyler stopped his search and ambled to my side of the room. "Help me move this crate where there is more room." I motioned over to a cleared area. The crate was about 5 ft tall and about 3 ft wide. Applying a crowbar to the boards, the front panel fell open. Inside, the piece was wrapped in blankets, and we gently removed them. There it was! The infamous spar box! Tyler and I managed to remove it from the crate without much difficulty. The wood and glass frame was intact.

Tyler said, "This is quite an elaborate piece of work. Look at the scene!" He described to me the different crystals, and use of the mirror and candle holders.

"There must be a place to open the glass door," I said.

Tyler examined the framework and found a latch that opened the door. "We must be very careful; we don't want to damage the minerals inside."

I used my flashlight to peer inside. I examined all of its contents. I did not see any coins or paper money in the scene and did not see a keyhole anywhere inside. "I wonder where the loot is hidden."

"Uncle, the money could have been found and taken years ago," Tyler said.

"I guess that is possible. But then again, according to Timothy's note, he mailed the key to America. Since I don't see a keyhole, there must be a hidden compartment." We searched the back, sides, feet and bottom of the box, and found nothing. "Tyler, I want you to bring Aspen over here and see if she knows the secret to opening this spar box."

Chapter 28 ~Aspen Listens to Tyler's Explanation~

After saying good-bye to Tyler, I walked back to our room. Dad was napping and Mom was reading. I talked to her about the events of the day. In response, Mom said, "I don't know why Mr. Dent didn't want you to stay and help look for the spar box. He seemed so nice when we first met him."

"I don't have an answer to that, Mom." About that time my phone chimed, "It's Tyler," and I excused myself to my room. "Hi Tyler, I said.

"Aspen," he whispered," I can't talk too loud, I don't want Uncle Allen to hear me. Can I come over? "

"Sure," I said.

"I am going to call you right back. Please play along. Tell me you are getting ready to go to dinner with your parents."

"Okay." Then a few seconds later, my phone rang again.

"Hello?"

"Hi Aspen, "Tyler said in a regular voice.

"Hi Tyler,"

"Uncle Allen would like for you to come visit. Are you busy?"

I followed his instructions, "I am getting ready to go to dinner with my parents."

"Hang on a minute, "Tyler said. Then I could hear Allen and him talking in the background. After a few seconds, Tyler replied to me,' How about tomorrow after I get off work?"

"I replied, "That will be fine." Then in a quiet tone, I said," Say my name if you are coming over now."

Tyler said, "That will be fine, I will see you when I leave work. Good-bye, Aspen."

I left my room and walked back to the den. "What's going on?" Mom asked.

"I'm not sure. Tyler is on his way over. Apparently he was at his uncle's house, but did not want him to know he was calling."

About 20 minutes, later, Tyler rapped on the door. Dad was awake from his nap and he and Mom were sitting on the couch. I opened the door, and Tyler said, "Sorry about the charade. I've come to explain." He exchanged greetings with my parents, and said," I would like for your parents to listen, as well." A coffee table separated the couch and matching loveseat. Tyler and I sat across from my parents.

Tyler explained, "When I returned to Allen's house, he showed me an old family Bible. There was a notation in it,

160

apparently from Timothy Sutton. He used the first letter of names instead of the whole name, but the note said that E stole money from T, and Timothy found it, and sent key and letter to T.'

"That verifies Timothy's letter to Thomas!"

"Yes, Aspen, it does. But, Uncle Allen is very selfish and, well, we found the spar box."

"You did?" I said as I touched his shoulder, in excitement.

"Yes, but let me finish. Allen," he paused, "and I examined the spar box from top to bottom and could not find a keyhole or money. I told him the money was probably found long ago, but he didn't think so. Allen has a lot of gambling debt. Does your letter mention money and a key? "

Before replying, I turned to my parents, and my father said, "I trust Tyler, I'll get the letter." He arose and walked to the bedroom and returned with the yellowed envelope. He handed it to Tyler, who opened it, and perused Timothy's explanation to Thomas. Tyler commented about the latticework, and commented that the drawer was obviously well-hidden.

"So do you have the key?"

My dad replied, "Yes, it is in a safe place."

Tyler replied, "Uncle Allen wants you to try to find the money in the spar box in his presence, but I am sure he will claim it. I don't want this to become an issue. I think the spar box and the currency is rightfully yours, having the proof right here," he said as he held up the letter. "I've got to come up with a way for you to search that spar box while Allen is away from home. I am going to get off work early, around noon, I'll come get you and we will go over to Allen's earlier than planned. He has an appointment, and will not be home until later in the afternoon. Then we will leave and come back at the original appointed time."

"Sounds like a plan!" I said.

Tyler stood and said, "Thank you for letting me come and explain things. I'll see you tomorrow." He said good-bye to my parents and I escorted him to the door.

"Thanks, Tyler, for your honesty. I am excited about tomorrow!"

Chapter 29~ Pay Dirt~

True to his word, Tyler picked me up shortly after lunch, arriving at Allen's house within 15 minutes. Allen's car was not in the drive way. Dad had given me the key, and I had it safely tucked away in my jeans pocket. I followed Tyler with excitement and anticipation as he led me to the attic. He pointed to the spar box that was pulled away from its crate. I wandered through the maze of boxes and furniture and admired Timothy Sutton's craftsmanship. "I can't believe it. It is beautiful!" I examined the quartz scene. "It looks just like the description in the letter. I turned my gaze on the lattice work on the bottom of the spar box. "The letter said that there should be two pegs, on either side of this carving," I said as I ran my hands along the bottom rim and on the sides. "I think I found them." The pegs on either side of the box were wedged in very securely. There was no play. "I guess they have settled in over all these years."

Tyler said, "I'll go find a pair of pliers. I'll be right back".

It wasn't long before Tyler returned and handed me the tool. I thanked him and began to slowly manipulate the peg on the left side. After several turns with the pliers, the peg loosened and pulled free. I repeated the procedure with the peg on the right side. It was a little more difficult to free this peg, but after multiple attempts, the peg came out. Nothing happened. I asked Tyler to handle the left side while I handled the right side and we simultaneously pulled down on the wood. Nothing we tried revealed the hidden drawer.

"Why don't you try lifting up the lattice work?" Tyler suggested.

"Good idea." Sure enough, the pegs had freed the latticework as the piece lifted up to reveal a board with a keyhole. I pulled the key out of my pocket, placed it in the opening and turned the key. I clutched the drawer with my right hand and pulled. It barely moved. I took a deep breath and grabbed hold of the bottom of the drawer on either side and gave it a tug and the drawer moved out about an inch. I gripped the drawer tighter and steadily tugged. The further out the drawer came, the more I realized the drawer was not stuck, but very heavy. "Tyler, could you help me with this? It is really heavy. With his help, the hidden drawer withdrew from the casing. An old, yellowed canvas bag with a brown drawstring nestled on a blue cloth, preventing it from sliding around in the drawer. I loosened the drawstring and opened the bag. I seized four half dollar-sized coins and held them out for Tyler to see.

"Those look like sovereigns! "Tyler exclaimed.

"I hope that's a good thing."

"How many are there?" Tyler asked.

"I don't know." I looked into the bag. "The bag is full, we will have to count them later!"

Tyler grabbed the cloth bag, "Throw what you have into this, and shut the drawer back. We need to leave before Uncle Allen returns."

I returned the coins to the bag, placed the drawer to its original position, replaced the pegs and shut the latticework. Scampering to the first floor, we heard the front door open. Tyler hastily tossed the bag into the hall closet as we rushed by it. "Let's get to the kitchen quickly. Grab a bar stool and sit at the counter while I grab some glasses of something to drink." I followed his lead. Just as Tyler handed me a glass of orange juice and pulled up a stool next to me, Allen entered the room.

"Good day Uncle. I got off work earlier than expected. Aspen and I have been waiting for you. Would you like some juice?"

Allen looked perturbed, "No. Not right now. There is no time like the present. Come on. Let's examine that spar box together."

Tyler and I left our glasses on the table and followed Allen up the stairs to the attic. When Allen presented the spar box to me, I acted surprised. But Allen was the one in for a surprise. Allen said, "I assume that Tyler told you that I know about the letter and the key." I nodded. "Hand it over".

I took the key from my pocket and gave it to him. "I have not been able to find a keyhole. Did your letter say how to open the spar box? "

With hesitation, I explained how to open the hidden drawer. "The letter said there were two pegs on either side." I tried to act like it was the first time I had looked for the pegs. As I found the first one, Allen found its' mate on the other side. "The pegs have to be pulled out". Allen and I pulled at the pegs. I hoped Allen didn't realize how easily they pulled out. Allen inspected the bottom of the spar box and, just like me, couldn't find the drawer. After a few moments, I said, "Let's see if that lattice work moves. Allen figured out that the latticework lifted up and found the hidden drawer. He pulled out the drawer with anticipation.

Allen examined the drawer thoroughly. "There's nothing here. The money is gone!" He was obviously angry. He looked at me and then at Tyler. Then his gaze fell upon the pliers that Tyler had failed to pick up earlier. He spat at Tyler, "You brought her up here earlier, didn't you? Tyler said nothing. "I thought you were on my side. You found the money didn't you? Where is it?" Tyler again stood there dumbfounded. Then, unexpectedly, Allen put his arm around my neck. "Get the money, Tyler, or I will have to hurt your friend."

Tyler went toward his uncle. I tried to pull away, but his grip tightened. "Okay, Okay, don't hurt Aspen." He turned to me,

166

"Sorry, I don't wish to see you harmed". Then he said to Allen, "The money is in the hall closet."

"We will follow you," Allen said. He motioned Tyler to move with his hand and kept his arm around my neck. We followed him down the stairs to the hall closet. Not knowing where the sack landed, Tyler fished around the hanging clothes until he found the bag against the back wall of the closet. Reaching down, he retrieved the heavy bag, and returned to the hallway. Allen gestured toward the umbrella stand nearby, "Set the bag over there."

As Tyler passed by us, Allen tightened his hold on my neck, causing me to gasp for air. Tyler guardedly placed the bag on the floor.

"Now get back in the closet," his uncle demanded.

Tyler backed away and stepped into the closet. Allen snatched the bag, loosened his grip from my neck and pushed me away toward Tyler. The door slammed shut, and we heard Allen locking the door.

"Are you okay?" Tyler asked as he hugged me.

"I think so, I can breathe now," I responded, remaining in his arms. We heard the door to Allen's study bang shut.

"What are we going to do?" I cried

"Listen, do you hear car doors shutting outside?"

I calmed down, "Yes!" A few seconds later, we heard the doorbell chime. "Help, help, we're locked in the closet," I screamed. Tyler pounded on the closet door.

Fortunately, the front door was unlocked, and we heard several sets of footfalls running into the house. "Aspen, where are you?" It was my Dad. We continued making noise from our prison. "Aspen, I'm coming.

Seconds later, the knob turned, opening the door. Tyler and I tumbled out of the small room. "Dad!" I threw my arms around him. Two policemen accompanied him. "But why are you here?"

Dad replied," I did some research, called a barrister, and explained the situation. He said that with the evidence you have, if there was money in the spar box, that it was rightfully yours. The lawyer happened to know about Allen's gambling debt. I was afraid that Allen might try to be forceful, and by the looks of your neck, I'd say my speculations were correct. I attempted to call you, and when you didn't answer, I thought something might be wrong. So I called the police, and asked them to meet me here. Are you okay?"

"Yes," I quickly explained the harrowing sequence of events. "Do you know the whereabouts of Mr. Dent?" inquired the older constable. "I think he is in his study," said Tyler, motioning the police to follow him. The first officer tried the door, finding it locked. Knocking on the door, he said "This is law enforcement, Mr. Dent. We know you are in there. Open up." When Allen did not open the door at their request, he repeated, "Open up, or we will have to break open the door!" Again, Allen did not cooperate with their request and he forced open the door.

Allen was ready for them. Standing behind his desk, he faced the officers with a pistol, "Stand back! These are mine," he said, while waving his gun at the gold coins scattered across the desk top.

"I'm afraid not, sir. These belong to Miss Blair, by law. Now, put the firearm down, so no one gets hurt." As a distraction, the policeman to the left of Allen continued conversing with him. His partner cautiously approached Allen from the right side of the desk. He caught Allen off guard, and quickly tazed him. He immediately dropped his gun, writhing in pain as he fell to the floor. The first officer moved swiftly and kicked away the pistol from Allen's reach, and handcuffed him. After Allen regained his composure, the second officer hoisted him off the floor. Dad and I moved to the desk to retrieve the coins. Numbed, Tyler stood at the doorway, observing his uncle's arrest.

"This isn't over, Tyler. I'll see you in court," yelled Allen as the officer escorted him away. The second officer remarked to Tyler, "Yes, he will see you in court, at his criminal trial."

Epilogue ~ Happy Endings-2013~

I contemplated the changes in my life during the past year. Tyler was correct that the coins were sovereigns. After visiting a coin shop in Carlisle a numismatist authenticated the profile on the coins as Oliver Cromwell, minted in 1658. He suggested that we submit them at an upcoming auction in London. Forty-seven coins were offered separately. Bids varied from $8,000 to $15,000 per coin. The final tally was $567,000. I kept one sovereign, and visited a jeweler who fashioned a distinctive necklace for me. I placed enough money short-term Certificates of Deposit to pay for college tuition, and the remainder I invested in stocks. I conversed with Rose Graham, asking her if she would like to add the spar box to her collection. She was delighted, but with one stipulation: She would return it to me whenever I had my own home.

Due to Allen Dent's trial, we remained in England for another month. Tyler, Dad, and I were subpoenaed to testify in court. Allen was charged with aggravated battery, attempted robbery, unlawful possession of a firearm, and threatening the constables with intent to harm. He was sentenced to 5 years in prison.

My parents and I returned home. Intent on exonerating my ancestor, Thomas Newell, I composed an article describing my adventure and submitted it for publication to a local newspaper in Appleby, UK, and Wytheville, Virginia. I conferred with Mom and Dad my wish to take a break from college and study art history abroad for a semester. They thought it would be an asset to my education.

I applied to and was accepted at the University of London. Appleby was about five hours away; Tyler and I visited frequently. Since he graduated from the University last year, he knew his way around London. We spend a lot of time together, visiting the local attractions.

Winter break was approaching. I was ready to return home, but I did not want to leave London because that meant leaving Tyler. We had grown close over the past months. Tyler took me out to dinner the night before I flew back to Georgia. I informed him that I decided to return to college and complete my degree. He surprised me with the announcement that he had accepted a position at the Atlanta Science Center, not far from Emory University!

I could not be any happier during my sophomore year in college. With a degree in Museum Studies and his job at Killhope, hopefully he will be offered a full-time position upon completion of his internship.

I was truly blessed.

Newell/Graham Family Tree

*First Gen: Anne Newell - first marriage - William Graham

Second Gen: Robert Graham m. Mary Thompson

Third Gen: John Graham m. Opal Brown

Fourth Gen: James Graham m. Anna Shephard

Fifth Gen: Oliver Graham m. Margaret Jones

Sixth Gen: **Rose Graham** m. Adam Evans

First Gen. **Anne Newell - second marriage - Richard Lewis**

Second Gen: **Hannah Lewis m. John Venable**

Third Gen: Stephen Venable m. Catherine Painter

Fourth Gen: George Venable m. Mollie Richards

Fifth Gen: Kittie Venable m. Fletcher Jackson

Sixth Gen: Elizabeth Fletcher m. Henry Newby

Seventh Gen: **Julia Newby m. Cecil Blair**

Eighth Gen Children: **Aspen and Austin**

*Anne Newell's Brother: **Thomas Newell**

Sutton/Lindsey Family Tree

First Generation: **Timothy Sutton m. Rachel Lindsey

***Second Gen: Kate Sutton m. Jackson Dent

Third Gen: Charles Dent m. Beverly Redd

Fourth Gen: Marshal Dent m. Mary Walsh

Fifth Gen: Dennis Dent m. Sadie Walker

Sixth Gen: Wilbur Dent m. Margaret Holman

****Seventh Gen: Geoffrey Dent m. Gloria Edwards

Eighth Gen: **Tyler Dent**

Timothy Sutton's brother: **Edward Sutton

***Kate Sutton's brother: **Timothy Sutton Jr**

****Geoffrey Dent's brother: **Allen Dent**

Rachel Lindsey's Brother: **Albert Lindsey

First Gen: Albert Lindsey m. Lucy Smythe

Second Gen: Archie Lindsey m. Betty Brown

Third Gen: Mark Lindsey m. Sara Kent

Fourth Gen: Herman Lindsey m. Susie Grier

Fifth Gen: John Lindsey m. Teresa Samples

Sixth Gen: **Hugh Lindsey** m. Olivia Knight

Acknowledgments~

In recognition of the places and locations in the story, I have listed the following websites.

1. Emory University, Atlanta, GA http://www.emory.edu

1. The Shot Tower Historical State Park, Foster Falls, VA

http://www.dcr.virginia.gov/state_parks/shottowr.shtml

2. Langley Castle, Hexam, Northumberland, UK

http://www.langleycastle.com

3. Killhope Mining Museum http://www.killhope.org.uk

4. Hadrian's Wall, Housesteads Roman Fort, Hexham, Northumberland, UK

http://www.english-heritage.org.uk/housesteads;

http://www.hadrianswall.org

http://www.nationaltrust.org.uk

5. St. Cuthbert's Church Parish, Dufton, Cumbria, UK

http://www.achurchnearyou.com/dufton-st-cuthbert

6. St. Margaret and St. James Church Parish, Long Marton, Cumbria, UK

http://www.achurchnearyou.com/long-marton-st-margaret-st-james

7. Appleby in Westmorland and Dufton, Cumbria, UK

http://www.visitcumbria.com

http://www.cumbria.gov.uk

Made in the USA
Columbia, SC
01 October 2018